De Couleur Pale

Brooke Harrison

I dedicate this book to my parents,
my sister, Sydney,
all of the friends who have inspired me
and those who are gone that I miss very much.

Contents

The Journal and the Problem

There are places in the universe that are unknown to us, while there are other places that are known very well. The Underland was an unknown underground place, and so was the Anybody City beneath the City. There was Ingo, and all of the mermaid and merman cities underwater. Now... they're as known as any regular city. As known as New York, or Chicago, or L.A. There are many more well known places. But then there are the remaining *unknown* ones.

De Couleur Pale is one of the remaining unknown cities. A city in the sky, De Couleur Pale has remained unknown for years. And years. And years. Well, not anymore. All of that is about to change, because reader, I know De Couleur Pale very well.

I live in De Couleur Pale, a place where the colors and beauty surpass all other cities, the architecture is unbelievable, and things don't normally mix with the World Below...until now, I guess.

Everything changed six years ago, one month after my seventh birthday. I am an amazing writer, and everybody knows it. Then, it was a good thing, but now, I think it is a dark cloud hanging over my head wherever I go...one that everyone else can see, too.

For my birthday, I had received an anonymous gift in a bright pink bag....it was a journal, with pink, purple, yellow, and blue clouds all over the front. It reminded me of our city, and in it I wrote about my life every day. I wrote about De Couleur Pale...it's meaning in English, (Pastel - because of the colors and sky and clouds), how wonderful it is and how it makes me feel complete and bubbly and wonderful inside. You wouldn't believe the way I was attached to that journal. I took it everywhere, to birthday parties, in my backpack to school, to bed at night, while other 7 year olds carried around stuffed animals and small felt purses. Not me.

One day, during that month after my seventh birthday, I took the journal to the outskirts of the city to write. I liked to write in inconspicuous places. Although the wall surrounding the city is a place that scares me, I had a good time that day. I spent two hours writing the longest entry in my journal ever. I wrote down every secret that I've kept inside since I was able to remember. I wrote everything I knew...from the colors, to the architecture, from the people to the history to what I knew of the World Below.

As I turned to leave, a gust of wind blew the journal out of my hand, and up, up, up over the wall and down into the mist, clouds and sky below. The journal disappeared and I never saw it again. It must have gone Down Below, a place where nobody but the great adventurer Christosky Columcloud discovered such a thing.

A Plane

"Creed, are you writing again? Haven't you learned your lesson?"

I stared at Marc and tried not to look too annoyed...even though I was.

"It's been six years...nothing has happened." Every day, we had that conversation.

"Yes, but it's only a matter-of-time before something does." The whole matter-of-time thing was not being used in the right context. Does six years sound like it's been a matter-of-time? I didn't think so. Marc was exaggerating.

"Marc, you've been saying that for..."

"Yes, I know. Six years. You've been telling me that for..."

"Yes, I know. Six years," I mimicked. There was silence. I felt ashamed for mocking him, so I broke the ice by saying, "It was a mistake. I didn't buy the journal myself; it was a gift. Whoever gave it to me would've been heart-broken if I didn't use it."

"But don't you think it was a little strange that the gift was anonymous?"

"Maybe it wasn't. Can you really remember six years ago when we were seven so clearly?" Marc shook his head and looked away. "Come on, Marc! This time, my journal stays on my desk, where I can only write in it sitting right here. It's not like the same thing is going to be able to happen."

"You never know," was all Marc said.

Sometimes, I think my own best friend might turn on me. You never know.

I spent the rest of the day with Marc, strolling along the streets of Pastel. Clothes lines hung in the backyards, and I saw many a face in the windows, open to let in fresh air. I looked up and saw little girls tending the flower boxes on the window sills, and Marc and I waved to our friends, playing tag and hide and seek in the foggy places in the neighborhoods.

We passed the town hall, the bakery, the bookstore...the castle, my dad's shop (he tested and experimented with poisons), and we even stopped in at a coffee shop to have a quick drink. I talked with Ashton and Heather, two friends of mine, and then we left. Time seemed to pass so quickly those days! I couldn't believe it.

That night, a matter-of-time came. It happened so quickly that I didn't even have time to really think about it.

Pastel scientists had received radar signals of a large object nearing our civilization. They called it a plane, a large flying object that transports people and goods throughout the sky to other places below. I'd never heard of nor seen a plane before in my life. The concept was so strange and unfamiliar to me. Besides, Pastel was already in the sky, and we didn't need to go any higher.

Nobody was too worried, but the news shook me. What if Marc had been right that whole time? What if I caused the end of our civilization...all because of a journal?

NO. It couldn't be. Whoever gave me the journal was the one at fault. If anything happened to Pastel, they should be the one to pay.

That night at dinner, I pushed my food around my plate and tried not to think about the news. We were having

Brussel sprouts, broccoli, and salad, so at least I didn't look too suspicious. But my parents saw through me anyway. It's a parent thing - after all, it's in the guidebook - know your child well.

"Creed? Is everything all right?" Mom asked. She pushed a strand of blond hair behind her ear. She did that when she was worried about something. That, or she would twirl a strand around and around her finger. I watched for it. Ah! There it was. She twirled the strand around her finger, then let go of it. Then she twirled it again. She was always worried about me. She was worried that I didn't have enough friends...that nobody liked me...that I would get into trouble...that my grades would slip in school...that I'd try to run away (where would I go?)...things like that.

"I...I'm fine, mom. No worries." Mom and Dad exchanged glances, but continued eating. (I didn't understand how they could - who likes Brussel sprouts? - but apparently they did.) Throughout the whole dinner, though, they couldn't keep their eyes off of me.

It was a couple of minutes before bed time, and I was writing...again. I was about to ask my parents if I could go to bed, but just then, my dad walked through the doorway. The phone had just rung, so I wondered if maybe it was one of my friends. Okay...okay, the only friend I really had was Marc. And maybe Heather and Ashton, or Stella up at the castle...But it could've been Marc, and my parents told him I was unavailable. They did that sometimes, for my sake.

"Creed. I have some...bad news."

"Bad news?" I didn't want to panic in front of Dad, but it was harder to hold it in than I thought.

"Yes. Bad news. One of the King's advisors called, and..." Dad paused, and stared out into space. "The King wants to have a trial."

"A trial?" I lowered my eyebrows, and asked, "About what?"

"You," my dad whispered.

I went to bed and couldn't fall asleep. I sweated through the sheets and had to turn on the fan so I didn't melt or something. I woke up and got ready for school, thinking all the while. I couldn't come up with a plan, but I was sure Marc could. I made a mental note to ask him in school.

I sat down for breakfast and stared out the window. My house sat right on the edge of the highest hill in all of Pastel, the most beautiful hill because at the top a ring of clouds surrounded it. A bench sat at the top and people were there almost every day. You would rarely find it empty. However, I couldn't keep my mind from wandering to the topic of the trial.

I spooned some cereal into my mouth, and took a bite of my muffin, but for the most part, I wasn't too hungry. I looked down at my white top and sky blue skirt. I smiled at the sight. It was so reassuring, so uniform and neat and familiar. I didn't want anything to change. I wanted Pastel to remain exactly the same. If the plane came again...I guessed we wouldn't be able to do anything. Our precious city would be taken captive, and nothing would ever be the same again. Even though I had a funny feeling things were going to change very soon anyway...

"I love you, Creed." Mom whispered into my ear.

"I love you, too, Mom. I'm going to be back this afternoon, remember?"

She looked at me with her deep blue eyes (luckily I had inherited those) as though I were from another planet, then shook her head and smiled. "I tend to forget that." I wondered what on earth she meant by that, but I just smiled back and hoisted my backpack onto my shoulder.

Marc had tutoring earlier than the rest of us, because he was academically advanced. Ms. Blue, the teacher, had offered to tutor him so he could get ahead. He agreed, and now we didn't get to walk to school together. For that I was sad. It was more than sadness, though. Random people had taken to yelling out snide comments at me whenever I passed. Sometimes I was afraid they might hurt me. But they were only the *SUPER* weirded-out people. (Most likely mental, too, and with a couple of disorders.) Most just sneered and ignored me.

You see, the whole 'journal incident' may not seem like a big deal, but in Pastel, it's more than big. It's huge. GIGANTIC. Pastel has remained unknown for so long that the people have gotten used to being their own little city. They've forgotten what it's like to meet new people, to go somewhere new and to have fun adventures. They want the sky all to themselves, and don't want Pastel to get overpopulated because of all of those who would really want to live here. I don't want intruders, either, but I think the people have become selfish and scared. I think they're cowards.

Pastel and Down Below just shouldn't mix. That's the only reason I don't want Pastel to become known. It's just not right. Pastel is almost like a fantasy place...a place of magic and wonders. Down Below was just...Down Below. Magic can't mix with something non-magical.

I kicked the dust around in the streets and tried to look like every normal school kid. I don't think it worked.

"Is that Creed? *Thanks!* Thanks for everything you've done...to *RUIN* us!"

I was thankful that was the only comment I got on my way to the classroom. Some of the others I saw just turned their backs or hurried into their houses. It had only just gotten worse, now because of the plane report. I felt like screaming...people had just begun to forget, and then the planes had to show up. Why me?

But rude comments and body language were not the only things I got. There were more people who were nice than those who hated me. They were the ones who stuck up for me and stayed by my side. In a way, I was like one great debate in Pastel. Possibly the greatest.

"Creed, dear? Did your mother get the cookies I sent her yesterday?" or...

"Creed! I haven't seen you in a while lately. Amy's been chomping at the bit to visit you!"

Those comments made me feel better. I loved hearing them.

I passed under the Great Arch a moment later, the arch leading to the school grounds. There were arches all over, leading to different parts of the city. Sometimes, the arches served as little bridges, connecting an almost-road above our heads. The 'almost-roads' were skinny ledges sticking out from the second stories of houses. They didn't pass along the front of the houses, though, only the sides, for the front was where the balconies were.

Balconies were very important in Pastel. If you had one, (almost everyone did), the decorations put there symbolized your status. No one really said this or acknowledged it out loud, but they knew it. So the balconies were lavished with beautiful chairs, plants, and pottery of every kind. Flowers and vines draped from them and hung over so that they were visible from the front door.

Sometimes, people had more than one balcony. The houses were tall and skinny in Pastel, and usually connected. There were at least three stories, so two or three balconies accompanied them. I loved looking at them and picking my favorite ones. This never got old, because people were constantly changing the pots and flowers and adding new things. Plus, the balconies were never overdone. They always looked pristine and well taken care of.

The only houses on the school grounds were those of the various schoolteachers and principals. I use plural because there were many schools. When you live in one giant city, you have to have many schools. We have a day care, pre-school, elementary school, middle school, high school, and college. They are the finest you'll ever attend...they have to be, considering there is only one of each and no one really gets a choice. (Unless they want to break the law.)

The middle school is taught by three teachers: Ms. Blue, Mrs. Blossom, and Mr. Vyne. They're very sweet, yet firm and they all know how to handle their part of the classroom. They each have two aides, and together, each teaches one of the middle school grades: 6th, Mrs. Blossom, 7th, Ms. Blue, and 8th, Mr. Vyne. They each get their own room to teach their grade.

Now, you can probably guess how many kids there would be in one grade. A lot. That's why the rooms are big and each teacher has two aides.

The 7th grade room is the farthest to the right, so when the building came into sight, that was the one I made for. I reached the class just in time. The bell rang as soon as I sat down. We have very big desks, and there is a cabinet by each, so I had somewhere to put my backpack. With so many kids, you have to be organized.

We were silent as soon as the bell finished ringing. We stood up for prayer and the Pastel Pledge of Allegiance, then sat down once again. I spotted Marc, two desks away, working rapidly in a book of his. I smiled. I knew how passionate Marc was about his work.

"Today, class, I want to discuss something that is...how do I say...a legend, or myth, in modern Pastelian time. Does anyone know what a legend is?"

More than half the class raised their hands. We'd learned about legends last year. I knew the teacher was just reviewing, so I didn't bother to raise my hand.

"Yes, Roxy?" I laughed to myself. No one would guess it...but Roxy was a complete genius. Not as smart as Marc, but close enough. She'd been offered tutoring, too, but only chose to do it some of the time. She looked like a tomboy, with long, curly red hair and scraped knees. Jeans were practically her entire wardrobe. Sasha was her best friend, and the two never left the other's side. They had many other friends, and if Sasha had a friend, they were Roxy's friend, too. Sasha was just as smart as Roxy, but not as outgoing. She was shy and quiet.

"A legend is an unverifiable story passed from generation to generation. A myth is a traditional or legendary story, or you could say an invented story or idea."

"Very good. Roxy is quite right. Today we're talking about one of the most widely spread legends in Pastel. We're going to go over it some, and when I make notes on the board I want you to copy them."

The legend was one I'd never heard before, and I'd heard plenty of legends. It was the idea that clouds could actually hold, carry, and transport items.

"It is said that in the olden days of Pastel, those who wished to travel would hop on a cloud and go there. What do you kids think?"

For the rest of the day, we continued to discuss and take notes on the legend. We had a period to discuss our opinions, and then Ms. Blue voiced some of the scientific significance of the theory. There wasn't much.

"I don't understand." Bryce, one of the younger boys in the class, spoke up. "If we're a city in the sky, surrounded by clouds, why doesn't someone test the legend? Why can't someone prove whether or not it's true?"

Ms. Blue and her aides, Mrs. Hart and Miss Ayre, laughed. "Bryce, sweetheart, what if the theory was proved wrong? The person testing it would fall Below and could die! People are scared to test the theory because of this."

"Oh." Bryce reddened.

The next morning was a day off (teacher planning), and I awoke to light streaming in through my window. I hastened to get up. Marc met me outside, and we wandered through the streets together again. We had nothing else to do, and for a change, I was glad.

We stopped at a small cafe. We each bought a muffin and a glass of orange juice and sat down to chat. I couldn't meet his eyes. I was the kind of person who didn't like to admit being wrong, and in this case, Marc was right.

"Are you worried?" he asked quietly. I nodded. I couldn't bring myself to say anything. "Don't. We'll be fine."

Marc was my best friend. Better than best. We had been buddies since we were born. We needed each other...he comforted me, made me feel at ease, and had a way of calming me down. I brought out the best in him. We were a perfect fit, like the last two pieces of a puzzle. There was another thing I loved about him, though...whenever I was down, he made me feel better by referring to my problem as one we both shared.

"Do you have a plan?" I asked anxiously.

"I'm working on it," he said with a sly smile. I couldn't help but smile back. There it was...the other piece to the puzzle.

For a minute we sat in silence. Then, Marc popped up.

"I've got it!" he cried. He held out his hand to pull me up. He smiled even bigger. "My plan. This is Phase 1."

The Trial

Marc and I raced through Pastel, bumping into people and carts and strollers. We knocked down signs and fruit stands and stepped on feet. Marc didn't seem to care, and neither did I, for that matter. He had a plan, and that was all that mattered to me.

When we reached my house, the TV was on inside. The news.

"Our radar hasn't picked up any signs of the plane, but we have a feeling it will be back. Whoever is in it was either very lost, or knows something about Pastel."

I noticed that the anchor woman didn't say *'somehow knows something about Pastel.'*

Marc gave me a sympathetic look and patted me on the back. Then he led me down the hall to my parent's room, where my mom was folding laundry.

"Hi, Mrs. Skye." Marc smiled his innocent boyish smile, and I copied. I had no idea how that fit into Phase 1. "Creed and I were just sharing old memories...and I was wondering, who gave Creed that journal for her seventh birthday?"

Mom's smile faded. We didn't ever talk about that birthday. We tried to forget it. Actually, we'd tried to remove all existing memories of it.

"We're...we're not sure. She told you the gift was anonymous, I assume?" Marc nodded. "That means he didn't reveal his identity. They placed it on the gift table in a pink gift bag and left before anyone could see their face...but it could've been anyone, for half the city was there, and they all left gifts." I felt the sudden urge to laugh. My mom was actually implying that Marc didn't know what 'anonymous' meant. Whatever. She had a lot to learn.

"Oh. Thanks! See you around." Marc pulled me out of the room and we ducked into mine.

"What were you thinking?" I hissed. "You know how we are about that birthday!"

"Sorry. But I had to hear what she had to say..." His hazel eyes glistened and he turned away.

"You already knew all of that, anyway!" I scolded.

"Nope. We learned two very important details. One I was looking for, and one that will help." He looked me in the eye and held up one finger. "One: The anonymous gift-giver isn't so anonymous. *He* was a man."

I was starting to see the significance of the conversation, but I waited to hear number two.

"Two: This man was at your party. He was present, even if it was for however brief a time."

"*Oh!*" I understood now. He was right. If only we hadn't burned all pictures from that party.

He scrambled to slide under my bed. Only his legs were still visible. I could hear him moving around, but I had no idea what he was up to. After a minute, he pulled out an old scrapbook. It was covered in dust and was old and tattered, but it was a scrapbook nonetheless. I stared in astonishment. It was my scrapbook.

"Where did you get that?" I asked accusingly. I had made it right after that seventh birthday, putting in it every photo I could find that had been taken that day. But then I had lost it, and we searched and searched but never found it. We had wanted to take out all of the birthday photos. For the first time ever, Marc blushed.

"Uhhhh...well, you see...I hid it here so you guys wouldn't find it and burn it along with everything else. It was still your birthday, even if it did bring on some bad luck. Plus...it was the start of our friendship. I didn't want to lose those memories just because of some stupid journal."

I couldn't help but blush too. I averted my eyes quickly. I grabbed for the scrapbook, but Marc was too quick.

"If my parents see that...I'll be dead." Marc nodded. He knew the seriousness of the matter. Quietly, we slipped out of the house. We found a quiet place by some trees and sat down to take a look at the scrapbook. For hours, we pored over it, hoping to find some evidence of the mysterious giver...a face, a figure, a silhouette. I was just about to put aside another picture - of me blowing out my birthday candles - when Marc caught my arm.

"Let me see that!" He took the picture gently out of my hand and scrutinized it. "Who's that?" He whispered, and pointed to a lone man standing at the very back of the crowd swarming around me in the scene.

"I...I don't know. Do you think...?" We looked at each other, and we both found excitement in the other's expression.

We didn't have time to get far, though, for that afternoon, my mom hurried out of the house and stopped us. Marc barely had time to slide the scrapbook and picture up his shirt. He was in the process of tucking it in (so the items wouldn't fall out) and pulling his sweatshirt tight around his body when my mom reached us.

She looked at him suspiciously, but seemed to forget the fact he was even there when she turned to me.

"The trial is to be held day after tomorrow, 9:00 a.m. at the castle. You'll be missing school."

"Mom, why a trial? I'm not sure I understand." Mom twirled a piece of hair around her finger and tucked another behind her ear. I noticed her sign of worry, wishing it was unnecessary.

"They...I think they're discussing banishing you. In their eyes, you've betrayed Pastel." A tear rolled down her cheek and she hugged me close. "It will never happen!" She sobbed into my arms.

"I hope not." I whispered, and buried my face into her chest.

She had Marc and I stay inside to work under her watchful eye. For her benefit, we played board games, watched TV, and did homework. There was no more discussion about our Mystery Man.

The day after tomorrow arrived quickly. Quicker than I expected. My whole family was upset, and we looked like wrecks. I just hoped we would be considered presentable enough. King Doulc was not a...how do you say it...kind man... but a stern, merciless one.

The King's castle was not too far away, so we walked. If they decided to banish me, I'd never be able to see Pastel again. I took a good look.

The sky was blue, and the clouds were fluffy and white. Hills rose up on either side of the street, and the houses wound in and out of them. Each house had it's own style, a little something that made the house special. For example, some houses were clay, some were rock, and some were stone. They were all different colors, pinks and oranges and soft yellows. Everything was a pastel color in Pastel...obviously. It was mostly because we were so close to the sun, and everything was beautiful and soft. There were balconies and turrets and vines swinging down past them, all the way to the floor. I stared at a bush and sighed. If they really did banish me, I'd miss Pastel.

We walked under an arch and up a small hill. I could see the King's castle in the distance. It stood tall and proud, and it glinted under the bright sun overhead.

I snarled. They had no right to do that to me. Okay, maybe they did...I could possibly result in the end of their city...but still...I was only a kid! Only a teenager, beginning those awkward years of her life. Only a girl, a sweet, innocent girl who loved to write.

As we walked down the narrow path leading to the palace, I watched my mom fidget nervously. I couldn't help doing the same thing. Dad led us there, stiff and lanky and silent. For a man who dealt with chemicals and poisons all day long, it was scary to see him look as if someone had just poisoned him.

The guards standing by the double doors opened them for us, and then we were led down a straight hall. We branched off and soon came to a large, circular room decorated with pictures of sneering men. Probably stuck up Kings of the past. Disgusting. I tried to look just as sinister as the pictures, but I think the worry still shone plain on my face.

King Doulc was whispering with one of his snooty advisers, but when my family stepped in, he straightened and shooed the man away.

"Welcome! Let the trial begin." He smiled pleasantly, but behind his fake mask I could tell he was really impatient...eager to get the trial over so he go on eating feasts and having celebrations. That was probably the only reason he liked being King.

"Will the defendants please sit, and the plaintiff please stand. Ha! That would be me, and I'm already standing." His booming laugh echoed around the hollow room. I didn't understand the joke. Apparently, his advisors did, for they joined in the laughter. "Now...let's begin, shall we? You, Creed Skye, are accused of betraying our beloved city, De Couleur Pale. Pastel. A city that has remained unknown for years! Decades! What do you have to say for yourself?"

I clenched my fists under the table and jumped up, seething with anger. My chair crashed to the floor behind me. King Doulc only sat down and picked at the dirt under his fingernails.

"It's *NOT* fair!" I said through clenched teeth.

"Any why not? Why would any of this be unfair for you...when *you* are the betrayer?"

"I am not a betrayer!" I screamed. "I was *SEVEN*! I had no idea any of this would happen! The journal was a gift, and...I didn't mean to. I didn't want it to happen, either. Do you think I would want any of my personal secrets being read? No! I love Pastel, and I would never give it up in a million years! A million *DECADES*!" By the end of my mini speech I had resorted to mockery. How could this rich, low down, snoopy, *snake* do that to me?

"Really? I find that hard to believe. You have always been a smart girl; but tricky too, and I don't trust your words." The King narrowed his eyes and looked down at me. His hair was jet black, funny, considering neither of his daughters had black hair. He wore a black cloak that matched.

"You don't? Well, what are you going to do?" I resented this last statement. Basically, I had just *invited* him to banish me.

"I hereby *banish* you from Pastel! Forever! And I demand you never come back!!" King Doulc was leaning over his desk, almost foaming at the mouth.

"Where am I going to go?" I thought I was being wise; witty, but King Doulc was already prepared with an answer. He must have known what would happen even before we got there. He was the King, after all.

"*BELOW.*" The word pierced my heart. I gasped. My parents gasped. I was about to protest when, thankfully, one of his stupid advisors rushed up to his desk. He had legs the size of toothpicks. I wished I could snap them. His crew cut made his large forehead and tiny eyes with huge glasses stand out. Geek. He was carrying a clipboard and was scribbling and concentrating so furiously that he almost bumped into the desk. At least he gave me time to figure out my next words. It was all basically a game; a game I needed to look farther into...so I could win.

By the time he was done, I was trying hard to contain my smile. But with the King's next words, it was wiped off my face. The Geek must have been thinking the same thing I had been.

"I...I..." The King Doulc struggled with the words. "I take it back. I have just now realized..." I was happy to see the advisor sneer at him... "...that if we send you Below, you might retaliate against me and share the secret of Pastel. I will not let that happen." The rest of the resolution was, I could see, getting easier for the The King to say. "That is why I have come to my conclusion. From now on, you will be followed by bodyguards who will watch you to make sure you do not escape. They go with you everywhere. Read my lips. EVERYWHERE. You will receive no privacy whatsoever...except when you sleep. Then the guards will keep watch outside of your home," he paused. "OH! And no more writing. Absolutely no journals. Your guards will see to that."

So the punishment had gone from banishment to bodyguards who would make sure I didn't escape. And no writing...I wasn't sure if I'd be able to make it through the next day or so without writing! I didn't say a word. Everyone was silent. That punishment was possibly the worst one he could've given me. For the rest of my life, I would be followed around by his tight-lipped guards, watching my every move. Never would I be alone with my friends, my family. It was agony.

"I must choose them first, so they will be appointed in two days. Until then, my soldiers will surround the city walls to be sure you do not try to escape." He let the words sink in, then declared:

"The trial is ended." He didn't even watch our reactions. He whipped around and vanished through another door, his black cloak flapping behind him.

My parents did not talk to me the whole way home. They only held me in their arms and stroked my hair, all the while sobbing silently. This was not the future they had wanted for their 13 year old daughter. Many a night we talked about my becoming an author...becoming so rich and famous that everyone in Pastel would read my books. I would build a mansion on one of the hills and I'd build another for mom and dad...but those dreams were shattered now. Gone, just like the journal.

Just a Friend

Marc paced up and down the street. He couldn't stop glancing at the palace, wondering if the trial would ever end and if he'd ever get to see Creed again. King Doulc was not the nicest of people. He took your words and twisted them. He said that the truth was a lie and a lie was an excuse. Therefore, there was no truth in his book.

Marc glanced at the palace once again before ducking into the coffee shop he and Creed had stopped in the other day. Once again, he saw Ashton and Heather discussing something at another table. He waved   to them, and they waved back, although they looked distracted and far away.

Marc had never trusted those two. He put up with them because they were nice to Creed, and that was about it. He thought they were hiding something. Ashton had short, blond hair and big hazel eyes. She was thin and tiny. She bounced around and looked happy almost all the time. Heather was older, with a curtain of black hair and dark, almost black, brown eyes. She looked Asian, but Marc wasn't sure. Heather was serious, almost too serious for his liking. Yet when she did occasionally smile, it was gorgeous. Heather and Ashton stuck to each other like glue. Some said they were foster sisters. Others said they were distant relations. Marc thought they were weird.

He sighed. He worried about Creed a lot more than he should. People were always bringing her down, ignoring her, and blaming her for Pastel's troubles. *They should blame it on the King.* He thought grumpily. He sipped some of his coffee and thought for a minute. He and Creed were definitely in a situation.

Yeah, they thought they had a picture of their mystery man, but what if it wasn't him? Had she even stopped to think about that? No, she was too blinded by hope. Marc didn't want to disturb that, so he didn't say anything. And what happened if they didn't find the mystery man? He knew they'd only have a couple of days. A couple of days to search the whole city of Pastel. You could search night and day for two weeks and wouldn't have reached all of the homes of the people of Pastel. The city was just too big. Plus - say they did find the mystery man. What then? Would he and Creed just shake hands so Creed could say: "Hi. You may not remember me, but you ruined my life 6 years ago."

No...they had to find this mystery man to chastise him about the whole thing. Marc had a feeling that the man might be hiding something. He intended to find out what that was. But it didn't really matter whether or not they found the man. Marc thought he had a plan. It was a bad plan - crazy, mental - but it was a plan nonetheless.

The only problem was that he didn't want to tell Creed. She would freak out. (At least, he thought she would.) He guessed it would be pretty easy to get away. There were no special guards guarding the wall. At least, that part was easy. How were they to get to the top of the wall? And what then? Just jump and fall down to the Below? He didn't think so. He'd have to work on that plan a little longer before he broke it to Creed. But really and truly, it was the only thing they could do. There was no other alternative, although Creed probably hoped there was.

A Trial Well Done

King Doulc was sitting on his throne, utterly bored with the entertainment he had been sent. Who cared about stinking acrobats anymore...in this age? Who cared about the stupid tightrope walkers in their skin tight costumes? And above all, his throne was scratchy!

"Your majesty?" A high pitched, thin voice called. A head popped up around the arm of the throne. Doulc groaned. Twitter was constantly 'twittering' in his ear. He had no desire to talk to him at the moment, considering it was Twitter who had ruined the trial. Who cared if Little Miss Know-It-All was banished Down Below? Even if she did spill the beans? Who would believe her? She was nothing but a child. A useless child. But then, of course, Doulc was forced to come up with another punishment...an even better one, thanks to his genius-ness! No 13 year old would like having guards following her everywhere. Especially when she started dating. No, she would despise that punishment for the rest of her life.

"Ummm...your majesty?" Twitter - again.

"What is it, you little twig? Can't you see I'm far too busy for your nonsense?"

"Yes, of course, O Great One. I just wanted to know if you needed anything."

"I'm fine, Twitter. Though of course I would do much better with a flat screen TV instead of these loony-toons."

"Yes, of course. I'll be right on it."

Doulc rolled his eyes and leaned back into his throne. He spent all of his time there - even if it was scratchy at times. He couldn't help that. And neither could his obstinate advisors.

"Your majesty?" Doulc groaned again. Although at least this time it wasn't Twitter. "Father?" The voice was sweet, like honey. Yet firm. His first and eldest daughter, 17 year old Katheryn.

"My sweet. Did you need me?" Doulc smiled. Ryn, being his eldest daughter, was naturally his favorite. You would have thought he'd love Helen, his second and youngest daughter, better, because she wouldn't take the throne when he died. But Helen was just too soft...and young. She was only 14 years old. Of course, she would be turning 15 soon. And Katheryn 18. Katheryn was going to make a wonderful ruler, like him. She was soft, yes, but she was firm, too, and had many ideas for his city (even if they were only for the good of the people).

"Yes, father. I wanted to talk about the trial."

"Ahhhh...yes. A trial well done, don't you think?"

"Actually...I disagreed with it in the highest."

"And why would that be so?" Doulc sat up straight and stared at his daughter. She never disagreed with him...never! She was his daughter, and daughters are supposed to *agree* with you, not *disagree*.

"Well, father, I don't think this whole fiasco is her fault! She didn't drop the journal on purpose."

"And how could you know that?"

"I just don't think she would've done it!"

"You can't just assume such things, my dear." Katheryn groaned and stomped away, in the process knocking the flat screen TV out of poor Twitter's arms.

An hour later, after watching some of his favorite cartoons, Doulc gasped. He had forgotten all about Creese's guards! (if that was her name). He picked up his cell phone and dialed the number 1. He kept all of his military men on speed dial, next to his advisors and The Quick Chicken.

"Hello?" Came a man's deep voice. Doulc explained what he needed, and Al, who was in charge of the city guards, sent his best men over to the castle.

They arrived in no time. The men were huge, muscular, and obedient. The perfect attributes for men working for the King. Doulc sighed and leaned back into the velvety throne. It would be a tough choice. He had to pick the best men...the strongest and most trustworthy. In other words, lugs. Lugs that wouldn't question him. He decided three guards would be enough. There was no way a little 13 year old could defeat those three.

Their names were Gib, Aden, and Alonzo. Aden was called Little Fire, for that was what his name meant. Alonzo meant Old or Noble, but no one called him that unless they wanted to be beaten up. And somebody along the line of Gib's life had figured out that if you spelled his name backwards you got 'Big.' And that was no stretch of the truth.

The three were so tall and square that when turned, you could mistake them for small hills. They stood undefeated, and usually brought fright to whomever they faced.

Doulc knew they would be perfect. With a quick flick of his wrist, they were dismissed. He would call on them again in two days to guard the little snob. Crade, Creese, Reed...whatever her name was.

♦ ♦ ♦

Phase 1

The next couple of days were spent searching for the Mystery Man. My parents had urged me to spend time alone with Marc while I could, instead of them. They told me our relationship would be the same...even with the guards. We talked about nothing secret anyway.

Marc and I figured that while we had the time, we should go ahead and do the search...for the guards and King Doulc would never allow it. Mostly, we approached everyone we met, only avoiding those we decided not to trust. I avoided my area of the city...in case mother was outside or was watching out the window.

On the second day of our searching, we came upon the apartment of some older citizens. If the day did not prove successful, I was doomed. Really doomed. My guards were arriving that night.

The first apartment belonged to a little old lady. She made us sit down and brought us tea and scones. She lathered the scones with butter, and dumped sugar into the tea. Marc and I tried to be polite by sipping some and taking a few bites...but luckily she didn't notice our still full plates.

When we showed her the picture, she squinted down at it and announced:

"That is my son! My sweet, sweet, son. He works in a bakery." She stuck out her chest proudly. Marc and I bit our lips, waiting for more information, when a plump maid walked out of one of the rooms.

"I'm sorry, kids. I heard your conversation, and I'm afraid she's wrong. She has short term *and* long term memory loss."

We left with heavy hearts, and weren't expecting much at the second apartment. A grandfather of a curly haired little girl lived there. The curly haired girl's picture was everywhere.

"Would you like some tea?" he asked as we stepped through the doorway. The tea from the previous apartment crossed our minds, and we told him we were fine. He responded, "Everyone likes tea. Especially Suzy Q," He gazed lovingly at all of the pictures scattering the room, then turned back to us and said firmly, "Out with you."

There were others still in their right minds, but none had ever met the Mystery Man in our picture.

There were two rooms left. Marc and I sighed. I read the doorplate. *Benjamen Sailor.* Hopefully the man knew our culprit.

We rang the little doorbell twice, with no answer. We were turning towards the second door when we heard a scuffling sound. The door swung open and standing in the frame stood a stout old man, with graying hair and glasses and a nice smile. He looked like he was maybe in his late thirties or early forties.

"Do come in," he said sweetly, and gestured into the cool apartment room. The two of us smiled and took seats on the couch by a fireplace and mantle. Benjamen sat in a cozy looking arm chair. It was an odd apartment...for Pastel was a very hot place and there was no need for extra warmth.

We then presented Benjamen with our picture and watched his expression as he studied it thoughtfully. I thought I saw a hint of a frown...but it disappeared quickly and the only one in the room really frowning was Marc. I leaned over and whispered, "What's wrong?" Marc only continued frowning in response. I tried to start a pleasant conversation with Benjamen, but Marc wouldn't say anything. Every time Ben turned, he'd start gesturing wildly. I couldn't understand anything he was trying to say. Then he did something I would never have had the courage to do. Yes, I may be courageous, but I'd probably start screaming and lose my temper. I happen to do that a lot.

"Why?" He asked accusingly. "Why did you have to ruin her life that way? You knew what would happen!" What was Marc talking about? Who's life did Benjamen ruin?

Benjamen only stared at Marc calmly.

"I didn't ruin her life. I only did what I had to do in order to make it better."

"You didn't make it better! And you've jeopardized all of the city just because of your own selfish reasons. I don't get it. You'd better explain yourself...or I'll..."

"You'll what? Tell her parents? Call the police? Just because I gave her a birthday present?" All too late I realized. Benjamen Sailor was our Mystery Man...the anonymous gift giver who indeed had ruined my life. I jumped up and was about to rush over to him and do something when...

"Don't, Creed. It will only make things worse. I think he's going to tell us something."

"I am. If only we could've gotten off on the right foot. First of all, let me start by saying I'm sorry. I did know what would happen, but I didn't know it would upset everyone so. I should have thought about it some first."

I stared at my hands. Here I was in the presence of the man who had torn my heart out. No more journal...no more friends...no more Pastel if the journal fell into the wrong hands. I wasn't doing anything about it. I was letting him explain. And he had just told me he was sorry. He was sorry? What good did that do? The damage had already been done...it was engraved in my skin, in my heart, on the gates of our precious city that was so close to being destroyed.

"Creed. Please believe me. I did the right thing."

"The right thing? How could this have possibly been the right thing?" A tear rolled down my cheek, and Benjamen pulled out a handkerchief and handed it to me. He came over to the couch and put an arm around me. I inched away.

"Every wonderful story has to be told. Every life has a journey that will lead them to their destiny...and yours has yet to come. I only interfered with the events I needed to...I gave you the journal; watched to make sure you wrote in it; waited for that one windy day when the journal was blown out of your hands and into the atmosphere that would escort it to the world Below. And now, if I am correct, you, young man, would like to journey Below to find that journal." Benjamen had turned to Marc. Marc turned to me and looked into my eyes anxiously. He was waiting for me to say something. Instead, I surprised them both by saying nothing. I was speechless. Marc was brave enough to journey into the world Below just to find my journal? I guessed it was something I could believe. There was determination in every line of his face, and his eyes were burning with an anxiety which I had never seen there before. (How did I know that?)

"I agree with him, actually. Now that the journal has been read, it is time you take it back," Benjamen tried to give me a reassuring smile, but I only returned it with a blank look. "Do you understand?" he asked. When I still didn't respond, he continued: "Your life impacted another. And now that life is impacting you."

"Whose life did I impact? Do you mean...?"

Benjamen averted his eyes. "Yes." He whispered. "Someone read your journal. And because they did..."

"They have impacted my life," I finished. I was beginning to understand, but that didn't help matters much. "So...what's the plan? Are we going to get that journal or what?"

The Necklace

Helen fingered the necklace. It was hard, cold. *Because its medal!* She thought. She looked down at it and rubbed it against her fingers. The tiny lock, shaped like a heart, was a shimmery gold, while the key was silver, studded with glittering diamonds. She had tried several times to fit the key into the tiny lock, but it didn't work. There was only one place where she knew the key would fit.

Who could she give it to next? She saw a maid around the corner and tucked it back under her shirt, so only the chain was visible. Then she hurried through the castle back to her room. She flopped down on the bed and stared at the white curtains shielding the door and balcony. She loved those curtains. Sometimes, when she left the doors open to let in the cool outside air, the curtains would flutter about and she could see outside for about a minute. She remembered countless times when she had stood out on the balcony, looking out over the back of the castle grounds. The castle was pretty close to the Wall, so she could see it and the expanding sky forevermore.

She did that now. Still fingering the necklace against her slim fingers, she stepped out onto the balcony and observed. It made her think about the girl...the girl her father had wanted to banish. Creed. Helen had been watching from a side seat. The whole thing had sickened her. King Doulc, her father, was mean and evil. But you didn't have to hear those words out loud in order to believe it. You could look at him; his clothes were the colors of filth and murder. His favorite colors were red and black. They symbolized death and blood, though he'd never admit that. You could listen to him; his voice fluctuated to pitches only of pure anger and hate. She heard it all day long...when he talked to Twitter...when he called his military men or discussed something with his advisors...when he talked to her. He didn't like her. And he loved Ryn.

Helen closed her eyes and tried to shake away the thought. Luckily, she wasn't jealous of Ryn. In fact, she loved Ryn, too. And Ryn loved her. But she wasn't there on the balcony to think about Ryn; she needed to think about the necklace. Her mother had given it to her, with specific instructions, *"Wear this necklace every day and never take it off. Don't tell anyone who gave it to you. If they ask, tell them it was a present. Which it is. When the time comes, pass it on to someone else with the same instructions. And when you do, don't tell them anything other than what I just told you."*

Strangely, her mother didn't tell her why she had to do any of that. She hadn't told her what it was for. Along the way, though, Helen had realized the importance of the matter...and understood that when given the necklace, you had to figure out the secret yourself, or else it shouldn't belong to you.

And then there was the fact that you would have to pass it on to someone else....when the time came. Obviously, it was her mother's time to pass on the necklace when she did. But how could Helen know her time? She didn't really want to admit it...but she couldn't help thinking it, and feeling it, and somehow understanding...that her time was coming, too. She felt as though she hadn't had it long, but she could feel it in her heart. It was almost as if the necklace itself told you so. Something was going to happen...soon...and she was going to need to give the necklace away before then, to protect it. And that led her to the final question; the unanswered one: Who should she give the necklace to?

That night she called up the family jeweler.

"Hello?" someone picked up and asked.

"Hey! Daniella, I need you to do me a favor." She could tell Daniella was confused, so she added, "By the way, it's Helen. From the castle."

"OOOHHH! Whatever you need, sweetheart."

"I...I was thinking...and I want a necklace done. It needs to be a silver chain, and on it I want a small, heart shaped golden lock, and a silver key studded with diamonds."

"You mean...?"

"Yes. Like their's."

"Would you like to tell me why...?"

"It sounds beautiful, and I want one like it."

"Alright, I'll try. I'll call you when it's done."

"Thanks!" Helen heaved a sigh of relief. If she had to give the necklace up, then at least she should have a copy of it. Something to remind her of it. Because how could her mother ask her to give up something that she had given her? Helen loved her mother with all her heart.

Just then, she got an idea. It came to her, like a small bird fluttering in the breeze, and she cupped it in her hand so it wouldn't fly away. Creed. She would give the necklace to the girl. She was brave, she was courageous and she stood up for what she believed in. Unlike herself, who hid when something went wrong. She couldn't bear to be that way, but there was nothing she could do about it.

◆ ◆ ◆

Phase 2 - Escape

I hurried home after saying goodbye to Marc and Benjamen, and began packing my suitcase at once. Okay...maybe not a suitcase...but a pack nonetheless. It was a drawstring canvas bag that I had received just that Christmas. I hadn't had a chance to use it yet, and I knew it was the perfect time. My initials were on it in aqua, and there was even a buckle in the front to hold it in place, just like a backpack.

After dinner I gathered everything I wanted: a flashlight, water bottle, pocketknife, pad and pen, granola bar, sweater, and a file containing all of the information about the journal. The pictures from the birthday, the dates and times and description of what it looked like. In the bottom of the pack I stuffed a small pouch with all of the money I'd been earning. I then fit a t-shirt and shorts into the pack.

The plan was to meet Marc and Benjamen behind Ben's apartment by the Wall. Once we reached the Wall, Ben would then tell us the rest of the plan, or: Phase 2 - Escape. I figured it was something utterly wild; otherwise Ben would've told us already. That or he didn't have it figured out yet. I hoped it wasn't the latter.

Sneaking out of the house was a different matter. Despite my guards, (who had already arrived by the time I got home), I would still try to escape. I had something in mind, and I only hoped it would work. Besides, Mom was a light sleeper, and Dad kept a gun by the bedside. What if he accidentally took me to be a burglar and he fired a shot? That would not be for the best. Plus, we had an alarm system in the house, and if I opened any doors, windows, or any other kind of lock...the whole neighborhood would be alerted.

If only I knew how to disable the alarm system. Then I could sneak out, get past my guards, run away, and we could get on with Phase 2. It sounded farfetched, but just then, I remembered something very important.

It was 4 years ago...mom had just begun to trust me. (I shuddered as soon as I remembered. I would probably never be trusted again.) I was nine years old and she was giving me and some other neighborhood kids a lecture on being safe. It was right after the other kids had left that she told me.

"Creed...this is very important. VERY, VERY important. Understand?"

Nod.

"You will only use this in case of emergency. Understand?"

Nod.

"Never...ever...anytime else. Understand?"

Nod.

"Alright. I trust you."

Cringe. Trust.

"I don't want you to memorize how to deactivate the alarm, just in case. That way, if you're ever kidnapped and interrogated, the kidnapper won't be able to get the information out of you. But the deactivation code will still be at your disposal."

Mom had used the old 'intimidating' trick. You intimidate the child so that they're scared and won't even think about disobeying. Although Mom is a little overprotective.

"The alarm deactivation code is taped to the bottom of the cookie jar."

I had laughed then. What mother kept her house alarm deactivation code taped to the bottom of the cookie jar? She had frowned.

"It's not that obvious, Creed! I'm not stupid."

"I hope not!" I'd muttered, but luckily she didn't hear me.

"I stuck one of those easy-peel-off stickers on top of it. All you have to do is peel off the sticker and look at the code. Take it to the alarm system and punch in the numbers. As soon as you finish, (the faster the better), PRESTO! The alarm is deactivated. What do you say? Is your mom one smart COOKIE, or what?" She laughed at her own joke.

There was not much time. Marc and Ben would be expecting me. I couldn't let them down just because I couldn't figure out how to get out of my own house. But now I knew how to turn off our alarm.

I slipped through my bedroom door and tip-toed out into the hall. The kitchen was at the back of the house, and the alarm system right beside the counter. My parent's room was right beside the kitchen. I'd have to be silent if I didn't want to be found out.

I slunk down the hall and past my parents' room. I heard my mom stir, and mumble something in her sleep, but other than that, it was an all-clear. The cookie jar was right where it always was, and I flipped it over with the flick of my wrist.

Crash! Bad idea. The lid fell to the floor and rolled around and around on the tile. With a final *'clink'* it landed in the middle of the kitchen. I stared at it in horror, wishing I had magic powers or something so that I could turn back time or make everything freeze.

"WHAT THE...?"

My parents. I was doomed. As fast as lightening, I picked up the lid and pushed it back onto the jar. In one deft motion, I peeled off the sticker on the bottom and yanked on the underlying piece of paper. As fast as I dared, I stuck the sticker back onto the bottom and pushed the jar back onto the counter. Then I ducked under the counter into the shadows. I huddled there, pushing myself up against the cold marble and squeezing my eyes shut, hoping maybe that would make me more invisible.

The sound of footsteps followed a second later.

All I could see was the edge of a blue bathrobe and the tip of a gun. Bunny slippers padded close behind. I stifled a giggle. Mom and Dad were hilarious sometimes.

"What the heck could that have been?" Dad's gruff voice said.

"Do you think it woke Creed?" Mom whimpered. Again with the over-protectiveness and worry. I could only imagine her twirling the strand of hair around the finger.

"Nah. Creed sleeps like a log. That's why we discuss all of our private stuff after she falls asleep, remember?"

"Uh huh. Good."

I put my hands on my hips and almost jumped out of my hiding spot when I remembered to stay put. I'd chide dad later when I got back. If I got back.

I listened intently as my parents roamed the house. Luckily they didn't go into my room. Must have been too nervous to even remember to check on me. A couple minutes later, after I'd been assured they had fallen back asleep, (they had come to the conclusion that the sound had been caused outside), I deactivated the alarm and slipped out of the house, ducking into the shadows before the guard around the corner could hear. The cool air hit me like a ton of bricks. I paused by a tree and pulled my sweater out of my pack. I hoped it wasn't even cooler down Below. When I snuck around the corner, I giggled at the guard. He was supposed to be watching the back door, but instead his head lolled to one side and he was snoring peacefully.

I wasn't as lucky with the other two. They were stationed by the front door. Hopefully my plan would work. Earlier on that day, while my guards were inside talking to my parents and I was getting home, I had stuck a dark pair of jeans into the bushes. I picked them up and slid them on. My idea was that the moonlight would shine down on my night gown and make me look heavenly, like some kind of angel or ghost. If the guards were even the least bit sleepy, they wouldn't realize it was me, and it would look as if I were floating. Then, I would slowly pull a sweatshirt over my upper half to make it look like I was disappearing.

It was go time. As quiet as mouse, I snuck out into the open.

"You are dreeeeaaaammminnnnggg!!" I whispered.

"What is that?"

"It's an angel, dude! Respect the dead!"

I stole away silently, while behind me, the guards continued whispering about 'the angel'. All they and my parents would find of me in the morning would be my note:

Mom, Dad-

I'm sorry. Really. I didn't want to do this, and I know you especially didn't want me to do this...(let alone think about it)...but I have to get that journal. If I don't, not only my life is ruined but the lives of countless others in Pastel. Your's included. Please don't be mad at me. I love you.

Love,

Creed

I hurried through the night and the darkness, hoping I would at least be second. I hated being late. I didn't want to be the one to put a damper on our plan.

"Pssst! Pssst!" I heard the sound before I saw who was making it. I ducked down behind a bush so I could hide. The voice sounded like a girl...not like Marc or Ben. I shivered in fright.

"Over here!" That was the voice, again.

"Shhhh!" I whispered. "Who are you?"

"I can't tell you that!" The voice replied. The shadow of a girl lengthened as a figure rose from behind a tree. I couldn't make out who it was, but for some reason, I had a feeling it wasn't a trap. But I still had to be careful.

"You know who I am," the girl urged, and she grabbed my arm and dragged me behind a building I recognized as Ben's. I realized with relief that I was close to the meeting spot. I scrutinized the girl's face and gulped. I knew her, alright.

"You're...you're...you're Helen...the King's daughter," I spat when I finished, and I think she noticed, although she didn't say anything. She looked at me and pulled me closer.

"Yes, I am. But I'm not turning you in. I have to talk to you before you go anywhere. I had a feeling you'd escape. How'd you do it?"

"Later," I answered. "What do you need to talk to *me* about? You're a princess," She rolled her eyes and removed something from around her neck.

"This is for you. I can't tell you anything more than this: Don't ever take the necklace off and keep it with you everywhere. If anyone asks who gave it to you, just tell them you can't remember and it was a gift. When the time comes, and believe me, you'll know when, hand it down to someone you trust with the same instructions. And don't tell them anything more than I'm telling you now."

"What is this? Some kind of tracking device? I see what you're doing, and you're not going to trick..."

"*CREED*! No, this is not a tracking device. Go ahead and look at it. Besides, my father's too cowardly to go after you. And I doubt his men are as smart as you," She handed the necklace to me, and when it touched my hand I thought it glowed. It may have been the light...but judging the way Helen looked at me, I realized it wasn't. I turned the necklace over and over again in my hand and saw nothing; no small beeping light, no suspicious lump, nothing. Nothing but an engraved *P* on the back of the lock, and an engraved *K* on the back of the key.

"Can't you tell me anything more? Like why you're giving this to me...and what it is?"

"You're the right person. And it's a necklace," She smiled before running off into the darkness.

I arrived at the meeting spot right on time...to find Ben and Marc already there. I didn't want them questioning me, especially about the new necklace I was wearing, so I asked a question instead.

"How did you sneak out of your house?" I asked Marc.

"Ummm...you know...I just...quietly slipped out the door. Nobody heard anything."

"Your house doesn't have an alarm system?" I asked incredulously.

"Nope," Marc blushed and looked down at his shoes.

"Alright! Alright, gather 'round," Ben ushered us closer. "I've got a plan. But remember...you guys already agreed to go through with this and there's no turning back now."

Marc and I glanced at each other. Ben showed us his parachutes - two large balloons with harnesses that could fly through the air as easily as a bird. He had no idea where we'd land, but he figured as long as we took it easy and were careful, we'd figure that out later. Then we all dumped out the rest of our things and shared what we'd brought.

Marc had brought a map, binoculars, a flashlight, a jacket, a book he'd gotten about the World Below, a very small and compact lantern, and some rope. Ben had brought a blanket, a flashlight and penlight, a pocketknife, an even bigger map of the World Below, two large sleeping bags, a compass, matches, and walkie talkies. We each got one and hooked it to our belts. Our items fit well into our packs, so we weren't worried about too much of a load. Ben had even brought some food. He figured we'd land somewhere near civilization, so we could buy food and drink if we needed to. He packed some bread, raisins, dry fruit, and crackers.

Ben then tied the parachutes together and harnessed us in. Marc and I were sharing since we were a lot smaller than Ben. Plus, it would be safer.

I hugged Marc around the waist and pressed closer to him as we climbed up the ladder Ben had brought. The wall surrounding the city was super tall, but we reached the top in no time. Ben showed us how to pull the cord to make the parachute billow out so we could fly, and told us some other tips in order to keep us safe.

One last time did we take a look at our precious city, extending for miles and miles. The place where we had grown up, the place in which we had taken shelter and refuge. And now we were leaving it to go on some wild goose chase journey in the World Below. The place we feared most.

But there was no time to let our fears drive us away. It was time to fly.

I hugged Marc tighter as Ben crawled closer to us. And with one mighty shove, we were off.

Hurtling Through Space

We were hurtling through space. We were descending farther and farther away from De Couleur Pale than we had ever been. The sky seemed to be falling with us, and all I could see for miles around was the endless blue of it. The pressure was unbearable! The air and wind pressed at me from all different directions, and I felt my stomach flip and flop and do cartwheels.

The only thing that comforted me at all was Marc in front of me. We were both screaming, and our desperate screams filled the air and space around us. I tried to glimpse Ben whenever I could, for he was another source of comfort. He actually seemed to be enjoying himself, as if he had been waiting to do that his entire life. What did I know? He probably had.

I was so worried that maybe the rope keeping us together would break. With the force of the wind and the speed at which we were traveling, the rope looked as if it could break with a single 'snap'.

I continued screaming until my throat was hoarse. Then I squeezed my eyes shut and tried not to think about the sick feeling crawling up my insides. I was free falling through the sky with nothing to stop me except the parachute's balloon, and it wasn't time to pull the cord yet. What if Ben's signal was too late, and we crashed into the World Below before we had time to pull the cord?

That was a dumb idea. Maybe the wind was getting to me. I turned my head as much as I dared to look at Ben. He was signaling something...was pulling his fist through the air, again and again. Was that the signal to pull the cord?

I tried to look at Marc, but instead my head was whipped to the side and all I saw were giant landforms, looming below. Their crags and points were sharp and jagged, and they did not look too inviting. The valleys between them looked desolate; bare and cold.

"MARC!" I tried to shout over the wind.

"CREED! HANG ON! SIGNAL!" Marc responded. His voice sounded like a whisper. The signal? So Ben's motion really was the signal? Did Marc remember what to do? Could he do it before we crashed into those humongous rocks? They looked like the sharpened point of a pencil, and even that sometimes pricked my finger. With those...who knew what could happen.

Just then, I felt a force greater than the wind and air and space. It clawed at me and we stopped free falling. Just like that. It pulled me higher and higher and I felt like I was in some kind of bubble - the wind was still howling around me, but I wasn't rushing with it. We were...floating! I looked up, and was amazed with what I saw. A large balloon was covering us, a balloon with only its top half. It was strapped to the saddle and catching the wind underneath so that we were still falling, but rather floating with the wind instead of having gravity pull us down faster and faster and faster. It was so cool! I smiled as I watched the parachute billow out above our heads, creasing and limping and then catching so much air I felt myself rise.

But that was not the only thing I was watching. The ground was coming closer and closer and if we hadn't pulled that cord, we would've smashed to our deaths. Now I could see every crevice and hole and every jagged ledge in the rocky landforms. I couldn't help but smile a tiny bit, now that the rocks didn't mean harm. We were safe and now I could really view the landforms in all their beauty.

The three of us landed 15 minutes later. Marc and I felt sharp pulls and tugs for a while as Ben steered the parachutes away from the dangerous spots in the rocks. Finally, he seemed satisfied with our location, and let us float down onto a long, flat ledge. It led into a very dark and sinister looking hole in the rock, and I secretly hoped Ben didn't want to camp there. After he gave us high fives for a 'terrific flying job,' he threw his pack into the hole and gestured for us to do the same. It looked as if my hopes were in vain.

Ben pushed the packs into the corner of the hole, which proved to be very small, and opened each one. He took out his blanket and the sleeping bags and spread them across the floor.

"Hey, Ben? What is this place?" Marc had found his voice. I was glad, because I still hadn't asked but really wanted explanations.

"I'll tell you in a sec. Sit down and get comfortable. You'll be cold in a matter of minutes, so I'd better get this fire started."

Marc nodded and led me over to the sleeping bags. "Hey, Ben, who's sleeping where?" He glanced at me. I giggled. He was right. It might be a bit uncomfortable for two boys and a girl to sleep together.

"Oh! I'm sorry! I figured we should let Creed have her own sleeping bag, and we could share one. Is that alright with you?"

"Whooo! Perfect." Marc relaxed. I giggled again.

We watched intently as Ben scurried around outside to pick out a bunch of rocks and sticks. He made a circle of rocks between the two sleeping bags, and piled a bunch of sticks into the circle. He ripped out a piece of paper from his pad and crumpled it up over the sticks. Then he took out a match and lit it, setting the paper on fire.

I was excited I remembered what a fire was, because fires were never needed in Pastel. It looked like we'd be using them a lot here.

The flames shot up quickly, and I let out a shriek. I jumped back, and hit the wall of the hole by accident. I looked up at Ben with fearful eyes, and when he nodded, I slowly crawled back onto the sleeping bag. I burst out laughing. What a scaredy cat I was! Marc and Ben laughed along with me, and we all made sure we were comfortable before we began to talk.

"Well, I know I owe you guys some explanations - so I'll try to do this to the best of my ability."

Marc and I nodded and settled in. I wrapped Ben's blanket around my shoulders. He was right. The cold hit me and sent me shivering, although it was somewhat better with the fire blazing right before me. Slowly, our hole was heating up. It was brightening, too, so it didn't look so sinister. Outside of our hole, the darkness seemed to consume everything. For the second time that night, I felt as if I was in my own little bubble.

"First of all, we landed in the *mountains*." He gestured to the beauty of the pointed rocks outside. "I'm not sure where, exactly...but I'm going to sit down with the map and the compass and figure that out soon. Second of all, right now, we are sitting in a *cave*. Caves are large holes in the rock formed sometimes by wind and water. It makes the perfect shelter and you can find them in practically any size. I wanted a cave that we could see the end of. If you land in a cave that extends farther and farther into the mountain, sometimes strange creatures could be living there."

A cave. Mountains. I rolled the words over my tongue and practiced whispering them out loud. I could see Marc doing the same.

"That's so cool!" Marc commented after a while. "Wow."

I wasn't so excited that easily.

"Ben, do you think you could find out where we are right now? I really want to know." I looked at him anxiously, and finally, he smiled.

"Sure. I need my map, the compass, my pad, Marc's lantern, the binoculars, and some bread."

"What does the bread do?" I asked, and tried to hold in my laughter.

"It quenches my hunger. Now hurry! I'm anxious, too."

I ran over to the bags and loaded my arms with the items. When I dumped them at Ben's side, he started at once. I sat down next to Marc to watch, hoping he would watch, too. Instead, his nose was buried in the book about the World Below he had brought. I peered over his shoulder and saw lots of words and pictures. I made a mental note to read it later. I was sure it had some interesting facts.

Ben unrolled his map and held it down with a couple of extra rocks. He lay the compass down beside him and looked at it quickly. He then made some notes on the pad and turned on Marc's battery operated lantern so he could see better. For a while, that was all he did; look at the compass and write notes. Finally, he put the pen down and picked up the binoculars. He put them to his eyes and viewed the whole terrain. For a couple of minutes he walked around on the ledge outside of the cave and took a long look.

"I'm thinking we're in the Alps Mountain Range," he commented. "In Italy," he added.

"Where's Italy?" I asked.

"Look at the map." I was surprised to hear Marc's voice, but he must have just finished reading. He crawled across his sleeping bag and around the fire to mine, where the map was spread. He scrutinized it for a minute. "Do you see it?"

I swept my eyes across the map. "There!" I cried, and pointed.

Italy looked like a boot. There were two mountain ranges shown. The Apennines Mountains were right down the middle, like a zipper that went all the way down to the toe. The Alps Mountain Range was like a cuff on the boot, spreading wider as it neared Austria. I wondered where we could be.

"Ben? Do you know where in the Alps?" I felt totally helpless like that - we had to ask Ben everything. I mean, you couldn't really blame us; we'd been living in Pastel our whole lives oblivious to the World Below. Sure, we'd learned about it in school! But they didn't teach you everything. We had no idea how big the World Below really was. No one (but Christosky Columcloud) had ever traveled there to be sure. It wasn't like we actually needed to know, anyway. Now I wish we did. For we were paying for it.

"I...I think somewhere by the border near Austria and Venice. All of us lived in the southern parts of De Couleur Pale; which I figure would probably be over Europe and Africa. I was watching the compass as we flew...and we were going east. So that means we must have landed over these mountains...the Alps. The only thing that will prove this theory is if we can find the Adige River. We can follow it down into Venice."

I thought about his words. He was right; we had probably landed somewhere along the Adige River near Venice.

Ben interrupted my thoughts. "Tonight we need to get a good nights sleep. In the morning we can continue our journey. I want you guys to decide where we should go from Venice."

"Ben?"

"Yes, Marc?"

"Ummm...you don't happen to know the person who read Creed's journal, right?"

"Unfortunately, no. The only thing I know for certain is that someone found the journal and has read it."

"How?" I could tell Marc was getting suspicious.

"When you interfere with two people's lives, you naturally feel these things. You can feel it when your job is complete...or in my case, halfway complete. My job will be finished when we've found the journal and all is well."

I studied my two companions. Poor Marc; he looked confused. I felt confused, too. How could the fact that someone had read my journal be good? How would it impact my life in a good way, like Ben said? And how would it impact the life of the person who read the journal? And the biggest issue I had was this: How could all be well when the person who found my journal read it? Even if I did get it back? They would still have learned all about Pastel, and my entire city would be doomed. I felt dizzy just thinking about it. The only hope I had of Pastel not being found was that the person who read my journal didn't believe it.

Marc seemed to read my mind. "How will all be well?"

"You haven't met the journal reader yet," Ben said with a twinkle in his eye.

"You said you didn't know who found it!" Marc accused.

"I don't. I don't know who they are, or where they are, or where they've come from. The only thing I know about them is this: They were the right person to send the journal to."

Marc shut up after that. You had to admit, Ben was a hard person to argue with.

◆ ◆ ◆

Gone

"FATHER! FATHER!" Someone called down the hall. Doulc wanted to scream. What did his daughters want now? Was it a TV? Or a new cell phone? Inventors were constantly coming out with brand new ones - with all different games and settings and ring tones. There were ones with flip tops so the text keys were bigger...texting was becoming a big sport for girls. It was soooo annoying.

"What?" He asked none too kindly. Katheryn rushed into his room, telephone in hand. Wisps of fine hair fell inro her face. She was flushed. Helen emerged from behind, her dress sleeves scrunched to her shoulders.

"Father! It's that girl! She's gone! She escaped last night!"

"She got past your guards!" Helen added.

Doulc popped up. He tried to breathe normally, but was too frustrated.

"HOW CAN THAT BE?!!" He screamed. "I sent my best men!"

Ryn shrugged. "I have no idea. She must be extremely smart. I took the liberty of calling the guards myself, and they had just found out she was gone, also. They say they were watching the house all night and nothing happened."

Doulc began to pace. He ran his fingers through his thin hair and ground his teeth, seething with anger. Someone was going to be punished for this. The girl couldn't have possibly been able to escape by herself.

Helen whispered something Doulc couldn't hear.

"What did you say, my girl?"

"I said that the guards did see something strange. They only told me." Doulc turned and stared at Helen. She was looking at the ground, apparently afraid to reveal anything more. Gently, he asked her what she knew. "Ummm...they say they saw an angel. A beautiful angel appeared to them and told them they were dreaming. Then she disappeared into the night and they never saw her again."

Doulc couldn't help it - he laughed. How ridiculous their story sounded!

"An angel, hmmm? She told them they were dreaming? How nice! I wonder how far the *angel* could've gotten."

"I wonder. But if you send anyone after her, father, you'll just arouse suspicion."

Doulc muttered something unintelligible. Helen was right, of course. If he sent a team of guards or military soldiers, who knew what they would find? If they did find something, they would certainly arouse suspicion. Why did his daughter have to be so smart?

Later that day, Doulc called on the three guards whom the girl had managed to slip away from. They pleaded their story, but Doulc did not believe a word. Angels rarely appeared to guards...especially ones like Gib, Little Fire, and Alonzo. It had to have been the girl - tricking them so that she could escape. To betray the city, no doubt.

The parents were mortified. They showed him the note the girl had left, yet he did not believe that either. He bet his whole palace the parents had been informed of the girl's plan and were involved. They were good actors, no doubt about it. Suddenly, he had a brilliant idea. *'Keep your friends close, and your enemies closer.'* His father had always told him that was a wonderful saying.

But what to do about the girl other than wait? What wonderful thing could Doulc do to save his city? After all, he had to do something. His subjects were looking up to him - they wanted him to be a mighty ruler. That he was, but still - then he got another idea. It would only work if certain people were willing, but it would probably work nonetheless. *Someone* would help him.

The signs were posted all around Pastel two days later. Doulc had everyone in the palace working on the project. His daughters made important phone calls, his advisors were keeping track of those who were willing to help, his military men were posting the signs, and the cooks were preparing for the feast he was going to hold. His best scribes were put to work making new posters and signs. Everyone in the city could write, it was a very common thing, but the scribes had the best handwriting, and knew calligraphy and gorgeous fonts.

The first sign came out like this:

Calling all Inventors, Scientists, and those who create...

Join me at the palace to eat and discuss a very important matter over dinner - a matter which would help our city a great deal.

When: Thursday Evening
Where: Doulc Castle Conference Room

RSVP: *Doulc's Advisors* (222-1222)

In a matter of days, 332 people had RSVP-ed. However, only 112 were selected. If you did want to RSVP, you were required to give your occupation in order to be selected. Many were only poor, wanting a chance to try and invent something useful. Those were the ones turned down. Doulc didn't want any beggars being let into his castle - that much was clear.

Doulc made sure everything was ready, and on Thursday night, he sat at the head of the table and watched the 112 inventors and scientists stream in. The inventors and scientists from the palace were seated around him, being the very best, of course. The room was decorated lavishly - from new paint to polished candle sticks and a pressed table cloth. The meal was wonderful, cooked by the best chefs that Doulc could find, and even the people were dressed nicely, in spotless tuxes and suits and ironed ties that matched the shirts peeping out from underneath. The beards were trimmed, the mustaches twirled into fancy points and curls, and the hair slicked back and washed.

Doulc himself had had his maids pick out his attire, and he looked very clean - with his ironed tux and golden tie, his pants and his pocket watch. He loved that pocket watch. It had been given to him by a dear friend...but never mind that. Soon the room was filled, and the guests were digging in and enjoying their meal very much. Everything was going as planned. Doulc couldn't have been happier. He glanced around the room and gave Twitter an enormous smile. "I think I'm going to like this, humble servant." Twitter beamed. If he had been called 'humble servant,' Doulc had to be in a good mood.

Once everyone had nearly finished eating, Doulc stood up and clinked a fork to his glass.

"I would like to make an announcement." He cleared his throat several times just to be sure everyone was looking at him. He did love it when people looked at him. "I would now like to discuss the reason for this very important meeting today." Now everyone was interested. They stared up at him with wide eyes. "I've wondered - how can we live like this? So...disconnected from the rest of the world? Why can't we see what's going on there, too?"

"That's impossible!" someone proclaimed.

"IF YOU THINK IT'S IMPOSSIBLE THEN LEAVE NOW! THE DOOR IS OVER THERE." Doulc scanned the room and fell on a very white, pasty face. The man turned away when he saw Doulc's gaze, but Doulc didn't turn. He gazed on and pointed in the direction of the exit. He was pretty sure the man saw him.

Everyone was silenced by this outburst. Only one person got up and left, murmuring something about the fact that Doulc was a lunatic and out of his right mind. But King Doulc went on anyway. His announcement was much too important.

"Telescopes have been invented. Binoculars have been invented. They are put to great use, considering we are much closer to the stars than anyone else. However, there is not a telescope I know of that has the power to show me the World Below."

Whispering broke out among the many guests. Doulc's scientists and inventors huddled together, talking quickly — some even talking in Latin. Doulc smiled and sat down. The people got louder. He frowned. Then he banged his fist on the table, causing the silverware to bounce on the place-settings. The guests were startled.

"Attention!" he cried, and banged his fist on the table again. "Is it possible?"

There was silence.

He repeated his question, and a chorus of "yes" filled the room. He smiled, content. "I am glad. It can be worked out?"

There was another "yes" chorus.

"You will work together. If you would not like to be a part of this, you do not have to. It is optional, and I will kick you out if I see you are not working, helping, or not doing a good enough job. I will put someone in charge and that person will report your progress to me. I know these things take time, but it should not take too long. I want that telescope."

◆ ◆ ◆

Helen had convinced herself that she had done a very convincing job. Confronting and helping her father's (now) worst enemy, had drained her strength. And Helen didn't have much strength to begin with. Then there was the fact that Ryn had been watching her like a hawk. Thanks to her little acting job, Ryn had become satisfied that she wasn't doing anything underhanded. Ryn knew Helen would never do anything potentially bad or evil, but most of the time she saw right through her sister nonetheless. Some said that only twins had telepathy, but Helen was convinced otherwise.

She was never able to hide anything from Ryn. Ever. But she had then. Just that one time. She fanned herself off and took deep breaths. It had taken all of her dignity to walk out of the throne room where her father and Ryn were still talking and to act as though nothing were wrong.

And now she was leaning against the opposite door of the conference room, where her father was giving his speech to the many scientists and inventors he had managed to drum up. He was always up to something. He had to be, otherwise he would go crazy. If the King didn't have a project, he was grumpy...although he kind of already was that way anyway. Helen knew many different secret spots and hidden doorways and passages around the castle. She had learned them from her mother. The only catch was that Ryn knew them too. It wasn't necessarily a bad thing, but if Helen was hiding from Ryn, or spying on Ryn, Ryn would know and catch her before she could get away.

Today, however, Ryn wasn't around to say: "You shouldn't spy on father! It's rude!" Oh, no. This time, it was necessary. If the King caught Creed, all was doomed. She might even rat on Helen, accidentally slipping that Helen had known she was escaping. And this whole telescope thing had something to do with Creed. Her father wasn't dumb. He knew he wouldn't be able to find the girl with the telescope...but there must be something he wanted. Helen knew him well enough.

♦ ♦ ♦

The Journey Truly Begins

We had a really good night of sleep. Me, especially. By the time I was up, the fire was blazing again and toast had been made.

Marc and I discussed our plans while Ben took a look through the binoculars again. We planned our route and decided to travel down the mountain to find the Adige River, which would lead us to Venice. From Venice we would find the Po River, and then we would travel into the Apennines Mountains. We figured that whoever had my journal must be somewhere in Italy, because the journal had to have taken the same flight pattern as we did, or one similar. How to find that person was a mystery to me.

In a matter of minutes, we had packed up and were ready to go. Ben scattered the rocks from our fireplace and tossed the remaining remnants. We didn't want anyone to know we had camped there...just in case.

Climbing down the rocky mountains was harder than I had thought. I continuously found myself tripping over pebbles and catching my jeans on crags and jutting pieces of rock.

We were like that for over an hour, tripping and stumbling and getting back up again, all the while checking Ben's compass to see if we were headed in the right direction.

After another thirty minutes or so of climbing, I could hear the rushing sound of a river.

We found a smooth slope down, and so inch by inch, we made our way down to the river. There, we filled up our water bottles and washed ourselves off...we were covered in dust and debri, and I felt extremely gross.

It didn't take long before we were off again, following the river and talking about our previous lives. I tried hard not to think about my family, but I couldn't help it. My heart ached for my mom and dad, but at least I was free of those stupid guards. I could only imagine their expressions when they learned I had escaped. They were conceited brutes, and once they realized *how* I had managed to escape, they would probably feel like complete idiots. Served them right.

We had just sat down to eat our lunch when I heard a sound behind me. It was a gentle swaying...so I didn't worry about it. It was probably just the wind blowing through the wild grass of the mountains.

I was admiring my new necklace. The one Princess Helen had given me. It was beautiful - there was a small silver key studded with diamonds, and a tiny golden heart lock hanging on a silver chain. I had already inspected each little charm - the lock had the letter 'P' on the back, and the key had the letter 'K' on the back. I had no idea what that meant. Only when I heard a crunch did I start to listen to the swaying sound more intently. I hurriedly fastened the necklace back around my neck. Apparently Marc and Ben hadn't heard, because they were engrossed in a very non-interesting conversation about the different fungi that grew in the mountain caves. I may be a tomboy, but I am still 100% girly-girl when it comes to weird stuff like fungus.

I turned slowly. At first, I didn't see anything. I look back now and wonder - how could I not have? It was standing there plain as day...watching me and waiting to pounce.

"Ummm...Ben? Do you have any idea what kind of animal that is?" I talked quietly but deliberately, and Ben turned abruptly. He gasped.

"It's a mountain lion, Creed," he said slowly. I gulped. I had no idea what that was....but a 'mountain lion' did not sound like something cuddly and cute. Or something I could make back off by saying, 'Bad boy!'.

"What do I do?" I could hear the panic in my voice, rising from worried to a high squeaky pitch. The mountain lion was advancing. The fur around it's neck was raised, its lips pulled back in a menacing grimace. It's teeth were white and pointy.

"*DON'T MOVE,*" came a voice so gruff and low that I screamed. Who was that? Had he been watching us?

Everything after that happened so quickly I had no idea how it even did.

The mountain lion lunged, and a shot rang out so clear and deadly that I froze. The dart whizzing through the air hit the mountain lion in the chest, and he roared in pain and fell to the ground. I thought he was dead. I turned to find Ben shaking hands with a middle aged man, younger and more handsome than him. His features were very pronounced, and I studied him very carefully. He had dark hair and sharp blue eyes. He had a square jaw, and was strong and muscular. Marc was laughing at him.

"Too suave." He whispered. I only smiled. Marc was so jealous.

The gentleman introduced himself as Griffin Lucas, inventor and archaeologist.

"Don't worry." He laughed. "I only hit him with a sleeping dart. He'll wake up, a little groggy, in a couple of hours."

Griffin walked a little ways more with us, and we told him our story. (A made up one, of course.) We told him we had come from Switzerland, and were on our way to Venice. We were travelers. I was Marc's sister, (ugghh) and Ben was our father. It was partly true. Griffin seemed to believe us, and that came as a great relief. Normally, inventors are suspicious people. (At least I think so.)

A couple of hours later, we sat down to have dinner and made a warm fire. Griffin shared his story next. A couple of times we interrupted with questions and comments.

"Well, I come from Rome, and I have a wife and one son, Andria and Cameron. I became an archaeologist at the age of 20, and now I travel all over Italy learning and speaking about its geography, plant life, and possible needs. Last month I started out on a journey that would take me across the country all the way up to the Alps mountains, to learn specifically about medical treatments and remedies. On the way back I planned to stop in various cities to talk about my newfound knowledge. Believe it or not, my first stop is Venice. From there I plan to walk to Genoa to rent a car that can take me back to Rome."

"How cool!" Marc cried, and immediately perked up. "Hey, do you know anything interesting about the different types of fungi in these caves?"

"Quite. You see..."

Marc's question sparked some type of special interest in Griffin, for he went on and on and on about that icky fungi that lived in the caves. He went from the slimy kind to the infectious kind to the kind that oozed down the walls.

I looked through my things and quietly took out the file about the journal I had packed. Luckily, Marc, Ben, and Griffin weren't looking.

Right after the birthday, after the journal had been swept away and my life along with it, my family went back to that spot to look for anything...anything that might have been left behind. I found one single journal page, though smeared and tattered and half-ripped, and I treasured it with all of my heart. Before I left I made copies and put the copy into the file. I took it out and read it.

...Today I asked Marc if I could come over. He told me no. That was interesting, since Marc never refuses my plea to play with him. In fact, he seems eager every time to come outside. Another interesting fact: I've never been to Marc's house. I've seen it, but he's never allowed me inside. Well, not that he hasn't allowed me, but I've never been invited. I guess it's just because we've never needed to go to his house for any reason.

He's never talked about his family much, either. I think maybe they don't like him. Or, even worse, they don't like me...

I wondered about the strange passage. Did it mean something more...? I figured I'd ask Marc about it in the morning...in private, so Griffin wouldn't hear and figure out we really weren't siblings. I'd be careful not to hint that I had written about it in my journal, because I'd never let him read it. I wasn't sure how he'd react if he did. Especially since I'd mentioned the fact that maybe his parents didn't like him.

A slight breeze kicked up as I tucked the paper back into the file. Just then, the file fell out of my hand and some of the papers scattered onto the ground.

"Here! Let me help you with that..." Griffin reached over to pick up a paper. I reached over and grabbed the paper first.

"It's fine!" I said a little too harshly. To cover up, I gave him a quick smile.

I hastily stuffed the rest of the papers back into the file. That was a close one. Thankfully, it was too dark out for Griffin to really read any of it. He turned away with a shrug and began talking again to Marc and Ben. Marc gave me a look, but I pretended like I hadn't seen it.

Before bed Marc let me take out his book and read some of it by flashlight. He told me some chapters that were really interesting, so I flipped to those and began to read. I leaned back and sighed. I felt so comfortable and at ease...I could get used to a life of journeying. I settled back into the sleeping bag and rested my head on my pack, my makeshift pillow.

I was just getting into a passage about the Adriatic and Mediterranean Seas surrounding Italy when Griffin's voice interrupted me.

"...I love you too. Tell Cameron I'll be home soon...what?...Oh, come on...you know I mean it...I really do want to see you guys...Okay, fine. 'Soon' as in, like, another month or so...ha!...Sure, sure...I'll be fine. Put Cameron on the phone..."

A tear rolled down my cheek. How I missed my dad telling me he loved me. I could almost hear his voice now:

"Creed, I love you." I wiped the tear away quickly. How silly of me. It had been my choice...my choice to find the journal, to leave the guards and the King and my city behind...and I still believed it was the right one.

◆ ◆ ◆

Misery

All that had been left was a note. A stinking note. On the pillow of her bed...her empty, empty bed. Apparently, she had taken that kid Marc with her. How stupid she was! Afraid to believe she was dead, which was probably the truth, Mr. and Mrs. Skye just talked about the punishment she was to receive when she got back. But in their hearts, they knew their conversations were in vain. Creed would never come back. And it was all that King's fault! He had given her those guards, made her believe that what had happened to her was something terribly awful and that she was a betrayer! It was at times like those when they thought of all they would do to love her when she got back, for she was a child who had been punished all her life.

In other words, Creed was the only thing they talked about anymore. No matter how many times a neighbor came over with a meal, or a present, they took it and could say no more than, "Thank you."

If they weren't talking about Creed, (which was rare), they were trying to have a conversation about the weather. That never seemed to work out.

It was a fine, sunny day when they got the call. They had been watching the news. There was radar signal of another plane, but luckily, this one was even farther out than the first. Mrs. Skye had just put a batch of muffins in the oven, and their smell wafted into the living room where they sat.

Just then, the phone rang. The phone had not rung in a very long time. Mrs. Skye cast a suspicious look at her husband, but he just shrugged his shoulders.

So Mrs. Skye hurried to answer.

"Hello?" Her puzzled expression changed to one of even more puzzlement. When she hung up, she was looking dazed, as if what she had just heard could not be true.

"Warren! We were just invited to live at the palace!"

"Where?!" Mr. Skye jumped up and looked at his wife strangely. "Are you sure?"

"Positive! One of the King's daughters just called, and she claims her father feels bad about our situation. She says if we go to live there, we will be provided with everything we need to live comfortably."

"Sweet heart! You need to sit down and I'll get you a drink. Think calmly and tell me what the King's daughter really said...if it even was the King's daughter." Mr. Skye walked slowly to his wife and put his hands on her shoulders. He guided her to the couch and sat down beside her. He reached for her drink and let her take a sip before he began to question her.

"What about our house?"

"They will pay for it while we're away, and if we decide to stay in the palace we can eventually sell it. The choice is up to us."

"Amazing!"

"Should we do it, Warren?"

"Ellen...an invitation from the palace is not necessarily just an invitation...it is an order." Warren couldn't help thinking of the saying 'Keep your friends close and your enemies closer.'

The couple tried to be modest about the invitation, but when they began packing and were questioned, word got around. Several neighbors came to help them pack and move furniture. In just a couple of days, they were packed and ready to go. The suitcases were already by the door. Someone brought over a tin of brownies, and others brought good-bye presents. There were new clothes for Mrs. Skye, and some new ties for Mr. Skye. They had to look nice if they were going to stay with the King. Around noon, they set out. Several limos came to pick them up, and they loaded them with the furniture and luggage.

As the limos pulled away, they waved out the window. Mrs. Skye tried not to cry, but it was hard not to when she remembered all of the memories she was leaving behind. Memories of Creed. Memories, memories...the good and the bad.

The limo was extremely comfortable. The seats were lined in pink linen, and there were wine glasses available for a drink. The waiter inside poured them fruity smoothies, and they soothed the nerves when they went down.

The limo was much quicker than walking. Not many people had cars. Only the King seemed to drive everywhere. There were cars for the exceptionally far places in the city, but for the most part, people walked.

The palace loomed above them in no time. The tiers and towers poked the clouds above, and flags flew from their tops. The King's symbol was a fluffy white cloud with a rainbow sitting on its top. A mighty spear cut through the rainbow and down to the cloud. It symbolized tranquility and strength at the same time.

The couple spotted a gardener trimming the bushes on the other side of the moat, and they saw maids cleaning the windows from the inside. They tried to count the number of windows, but there were just too many. In a minute their limo had pulled up outside the gate. The limos following them drove around the back of the large estate. The driver assured them that they would get their things back in no time. The other limo drivers were in charge of unpacking.

As soon as they were helped out of the limo with the few things they had chosen to take with them personally, a servant met them outside to escort them in. With a quick hand gesture, the gates were opened. The servant led them through and onto a gravel path.

Mrs. Skye tried not to stare. Everything was so beautiful!

Before they knew it, they were inside the palace. Nobody...unless they were there for a trial or were royal family...went into the palace. It seemed like too much. What a privilege!

"Let me show you to your room. The King has invited you to dinner, so he knows you would probably like to unpack and prepare. I hope you enjoy yourselves." He smiled at them, and they smiled back, uneasily. They hadn't smiled in a long time. It felt strange. Especially without Creed there to smile along with them.

The walls of the castle were adorned in intricate patterns and paintings. Many showed scenes of Pastel history, or places within the city. The ceilings had chandeliers in gold, and the carpet was a rich garnet. Everything was exquisite. Amazing and wonderful. They were led up several flights of steps, with golden banisters and carpets on every flight.

Finally, they stopped on a flight of stairs leading to a desolate hallway. It seemed to the couple the only one not swarming with maids and servants.

"The hallway leads to your own private quarters." The servant explained. "We have provided a small kitchen, laundry room, and storage house. There are two bedrooms and bathrooms. I hope you like it. We have only provided these things in case you value your privacy. You are more than welcome to have the maids wash your clothes and do your laundry, and cook your meals. The rooms have beautiful views, and in each one there is a telephone and directory in which you can find all of the numbers of the city. Included are the King's number, the kitchen telephone, the laundry room, and maid's quarters. Your things will be delivered to the hallway. The servants bringing it up will move it into your room for you. That is, if you still want it. The rooms are furnished."

Mr. and Mrs. Skye were speechless. How could this be? Had all of this really just happened?

The servant left a minute later, and they peeked into their quarters. The bedrooms looked so comfortable that Mrs. Skye thought she might take a nap right then and there. They picked the room they liked the best, and began moving things around the way they liked them. Eventually, the rest of their luggage was delivered and they unpacked.

The bed was a four poster, and their old bed went into the storage room. Most of their old things went into the storage room. They made the storage room into a sort of guest bedroom, although they knew it would be rare to have any guests. The dresser was carved with professional designs, and in it they folded their clothes and belongings. There was a closet, a quite large one, with shelves and hangers and drawers all in one. The ceiling was painted with clouds, and the walls were a soft blue. The curtains, when drawn, did indeed reveal a magnificent view.

Mrs. Skye was delighted to find the bathroom fully stocked with slippers, bathrobes, and shower caps. It was so much like a dream that it was too much to take in.

Just then, there was a knock on the door.

◆ ◆ ◆

Discussion

A couple of mornings later, I awoke to find I was the first one up...no, second. Marc's sleeping bag now only held Ben. Griffin was still sleeping peacefully in his sleeping bag, and Marc was nowhere to be found.

"Marc?" I called out softly. "Marc?" I looked around the camp, but still there was no sign of him. I got up and pulled on my sweater. It was chilly. That day we planned to break away from the Adige River to reach Venice.

I stretched and walked over to the river, flowing silently alongside our camp. I washed my face and hands and smoothed back my tangled hair. So much for a hairbrush.

I was about to walk back to the sleeping bags to find Marc's book and read some more, figuring Marc had probably gone on a scouting adventure, when I caught sight of a figure sitting some distance away.

Cautiously, I approached from the back. It was Marc, sitting silently on a giant rock. He had his head in his hand and his elbow was resting on his leg. He was staring off into space. He was clutching something, but I couldn't see what. As I got closer...I could make out what it was: a piece of paper, waving in the breeze.

I caught my breath. I had a feeling I knew what the paper was...but I wanted desperately to be wrong.

"Marc? Marc..."

"Go away, Creed."

"NO." I was stung by his reply, but I refused to follow his order. I went to stand in front of him, but he looked away as I met his eyes.

"Creed, I'm serious. I want to be alone. Please, go away. I know I've never said this to you before, but if you're a good friend, you'd do it."

"Marc, I don't understand. How did you get that journal entry?"

"It was on the ground by my sleeping bag. It must have blown out of the file when you shut it the other night."

I gulped. My remarks about Marc's parents must have really hurt him. I didn't mean anything by them; I was only seven. Seven. I hated that age. I hated that number. Some people called it lucky, but I thought maybe it was a curse.

"Marc, I'm sorry. I didn't want to hurt you."

"Creed, I know. It's...it's not that," Marc said softly.

"Look, if you're missing your parents, I feel the same way...that can be fixed! I can help you!"

"NO YOU CAN'T!" he snapped. "That's just it, Creed! I have no parents! They died!"

I stepped back. My mouth fell open and I stared at Marc.

"When?" I whispered.

"Six years ago," he whispered back. "I barely knew them, though. My nanny took care of me most of the time...but she died, too."

I couldn't believe it. All that time, all of our years together...and Marc had been lying. He had no parents. No house, no place to stay...and he never told me, when somehow, I could've figured out a way to help him. I could've done something. Anything.

"I...I..." I had no idea what to say.

"Here." Marc thrust the paper into my hand and put his hands over his face. I didn't feel like talking anymore. I ran. I ran back to the camp and curled up into a ball in my sleeping bag. I rocked myself back and forth, back and forth. Then I cried myself to sleep.

Ben woke me up several hours later. I had slept for another three hours. I made sure to wash my face in the river before he could see the tear stains, but from my expression and Marc's, I could tell he suspected something.

The rest of the day was uneventful. Marc and I didn't speak to one another, and I kept close to Ben, making sure to ask him non-stop questions to get my mind off of what I really wanted to think about. By that evening we had reached the outskirts of Venice.

Griffin, unlike Ben, didn't realize what was going on and was still as cheerful and 'suave' as ever. He led us to a gondola and found us an inn to stay at for the night.

When we reached the inn, he smiled and said:

"I must part with you here, but I hope one day we will meet again. I must now go prepare for my first presentation to the dear people of Venice." And with that, Griffin stepped back into the gondola and waved as the boat pulled away from the dock. We waved back.

That night, we discussed a plan to find the kid with the journal. We couldn't go around asking:

"Hey, have any of you seen a journal fall out of the sky lately?" No, we definitely couldn't do that.

"So...what should we say?" I asked Ben.

"I'm not sure. I'm thinking maybe something like, 'Are there any journals sold around here?' That might spark someone's memory, and hopefully they'll tell us about someone who found a journal."

"*My* journal," I corrected him.

"I was also thinking it would depend on when and where the journal fell. If it fell into the city somewhere in plain sight, it would probably be in older newspaper and magazine articles. If not, then whoever found it must have kept it a secret until now."

"You're right!" Ben and I began bouncing up and down excitedly, until Marc pointed out,

"And where exactly are we supposed to find magazines and newspapers from seven years ago?"

"I...I don't know."

"Right." Marc turned away and began reading that stupid book of his. I felt like chucking it out the window...it was his way of avoiding me. You know, I probably should have done that. Sometime when he wasn't looking...

"Creed? Are you listening to me?" I snapped to it when I heard Ben's voice.

"Huh?"

"We were saying it was time to get going."

"Really? Oh, well...right. I totally agree." I nodded, then stood up when they did. It was time to go find that journal. It was what we had come for, right?

Progress

It had been two weeks. The King had been restless, waiting for news of his telescope. If those dumb geeks didn't finish soon, he was going to go insane. Yet he had to appear patient, because if he rushed the geniuses, they might mess up - and he could not afford a mistake. It was too late for that. He didn't expect something with which he could spot the little escapee, but he was curious about the World Below nonetheless. He could spy on those planes, or whatever you called them, and spot them coming before the radar picked them up. He sent Helen down to the lab twice, because for a 14 year old she was quite tiny and didn't arouse suspicion. She was gentle and the Einsteins probably didn't think she was really spying on them. Helen had even called the parents of the little runaway to invite them to stay at the palace. He had to keep them close by...

Helen didn't like spying, it was too dishonest for her, but she knew it had to be done and she did it. She reported to him at lunch time, telling him all of the latest news and setbacks.

He had the lab specially prepared. It used to be the storage room, a quite large one, but there were so many unused rooms in the palace that he moved the boxes into one of them upstairs. The lab was under the palace, and it was one big room. He had installed lights in every nook and cranny of the place so it would be well lit. Using the suggestions of the dorks, he put in lab tables and shelves and beakers and microscopes. He drilled small hooks into the wall so the nerds could hang their lab coats. And by 'he', I mean his Advisors. A King is a King is a King. The reason they have maids and servants and advisors is to use them to do the things they didn't feel like doing. That was an essential rule of King-hood, and King Doulc followed it quite well.

Now he was eating lunch, and Helen still hadn't shown up. Finally, he called to one of his servants standing in the doorway and asked him to call down to the science lab. Helen was sure to be there.

"I need to see her right now." King Doulc said. "Get her out of that brainiac room. I need her!" Actually, he didn't *need* anyone, but in that case, he had to say it. It was the only way she'd come running. As if to prove his case, she hurried into the dining room fifteen minutes later.

She ran her hand over her brow and sat down with a plunk next to him. Then she ate. That was the thing about her - whereas Katheryn knew not to waste his time - Helen just sat there and told him the news when she was ready. She was not one to be rushed. But today, she didn't even utter a word. Not even once she had finished lunch. Instead, she asked,

"You called for me?"

"Yes, I called for you! You were supposed to be here in time for lunch! To give me news!"

"I was? Really? And when did we make that appointment?" Helen looked him in the eye. She never seemed to be afraid of him.

"We've made that appointment *several times*, Helen! Don't act like you don't know what I'm talking about!"

"Father, I know lunch time is the normal reporting hour, but did we ever say so? Did you ever call me or tell me that today I needed to be here especially?" She didn't even wait for his response. "I didn't think so."

"I am the King! You do not speak to me that way!"

"You are my father."

"UUUGGGHHH!"

"Father! Do not get so upset!"

"Do you have news?" Doulc tried to ask calmly. Instead, it came out sounding like a kind of threat.

"As a matter of fact, I do. Several things have been stolen from the lab." Helen leaned back in her chair and signaled to the servant. She asked him for more grapes. How could she ask for more grapes when they were discussing such a matter? The lab, and her reports, were the most important things to the King at that time! She needed to continue before he exploded in annoyance. Yet she remained as cool and collected as ever.

Doulc stood up and began to pace the room. It was a long room, so it took him a while to reach the end, but Helen could still hear him grinding his teeth. He did that whenever he was mad about something.

How could this happen to him? Those prodigies had a project to finish...and if their materials continued to disappear, how could they go on? Doulc growled. He'd have to go down to the lab himself.

A couple of hours later, after laboring down the many flights of steps it took to get there, King Doulc found himself standing in the science lab, surrounded by the whizzes he was trusting with his invention. They were leaning over tables and glancing at microscopes and scraps of medal with their bug-eyed glasses. At least Doulc wasn't too surprised. He had expected as much. The head of the project, his lead scientist and inventor, hurried over the moment he spotted him on the landing.

"Your highness!" He bowed his head before continuing, letting his hair fall into his eyes. "I'm sure you've heard..."

"I haven't heard a thing." Doulc was a good liar. He could fool anybody.

"Ummm..." Mack gulped, "So you didn't hear? Well...you see...some of our...well, essential items...have...they've disappeared." Poor guy. He looked scared to death. It probably wasn't a fun job having to tell your boss about a mishap. Especially if the boss was King Doulc. Because, most likely, he'd take it out on you.

While Doulc was still screaming at Mack, Helen slunk into the lab herself. She...Helen...knew who had stolen the items. It was one of the scientists, scared and afraid for the fate of his colleagues. Helen had assured him her father wouldn't use the experiment for evil, but the guy wanted a new King anyway. He claimed he wasn't paid enough. Helen was scared, she'd admit that much. What if this guy went all the way to get his wish? What would happen to her father's experiment? There was only one way to find out, and that was to keep doing what she had been doing for weeks.

The Gondoliers

Several hours later, I found myself on the canals of Venice, staring out at all of the passing gondolas. Marc was in one right beside me, and Ben in another farther ahead. We were searching for possible suspects. Well, not exactly suspects...you know what I mean. We had convinced the gondoliers to leave their gondolas to find some stolen items...items they'd never find. You see, it went a little something like this:

Gondoliers: "And how may we help you?"

Ben: "We were wondering if you would take us on a sightseeing trip...we're tourists...and, well, we want to see Venice in all it's glory!"

As Ben was explaining our journey (using the same fake story he had told Griffin), I stepped away aimlessly, pretending as if I were only enjoying the scenery. Which I was, while Marc, who we had told not to approach the gondolas with us, had been trailing behind. When I tapped my foot on the rough stones of the sidewalk, our signal, Marc jumped forward and grabbed my golden bracelet off of my wrist. When he was a good distance away, I yelled (only loud enough for the gondoliers and Ben to hear):

"Hey! That boy took my bracelet! After him!"

Gondoliers: "We will catch him for you, Miss!" The natives of the city seemed willing to do anything for the tourists and visitors, even if it included running pell-mell after fake thieves.

We had already investigated the alleyway in which we had come from, and because the only way you could get around in Venice was by gondola and there were no streets, Marc had to find a place to hide among the houses. We finally found a staircase with a thick flower pot on the small landing. Marc was to run up the stairs and crouch behind the flower pot.

Our ruse worked, for a minute later, Marc slipped back to join us. He slipped my bracelet back onto my wrist. He flashed me a smile before stepping away.

"Quick! Get the gondolas!" We hopped into each one and paddled away quickly. You may call it stealing, but I call it 'borrowing in a time of need.'

I was happy there were no other gondolas around, but still, it was only a matter of time before the gondoliers came back, or worse, someone recognized that we weren't the gondoliers. (We weren't even Italian...so it wouldn't be too hard to figure that out.)

Now we were posing as the gondoliers, waiting for someone (anyone) to hail us over to take them somewhere. We claimed we were new and didn't quite know where we were, but it was an easy way to find out stuff.

All we had to do was ask: "Do you keep a journal?"

If they said no, I pulled them over and told them we had reached their destination. Then hopefully they realized they were lost and got another gondola to take them to the place they really needed to go.

"HEY! *You there!* Over here!" I turned at the sound of a voice. A gruff man, perhaps in his late 30s, was standing on the narrow boardwalk. He was holding a beer bottle in his hand, and when I cautiously began turning the gondola towards him, he burped and let out a hearty laugh. I could practically feel Marc's eyes burning into my back, could practically hear his voice saying: "DON'T do it." But since when have I listened to Marc?

"The name's Kub. Short for...wait...I can't remember. I'm going...nah! Just let me off anywhere." He waved his hand and smiled. His teeth were a yellowish tinge, and I could smell his putrid breath. I almost fell out of the boat it smelled so bad. I wondered if he was of true Italian descent - but I didn't have time to ask him questions like that.

"Do you keep a journal?" I asked as we pulled out into the canal. I already knew the answer...but even if I did, I still needed something to keep pleasant conversation. People were expecting me to sing Italian songs at the top of my lungs and I already couldn't do that much. I at least needed pleasant conversation to keep the people happy.

"Nah. Too boring...can't barely even write my name."

"All righty then...that will be all for today. Here we go..." I began to point the gondola towards the boardwalk. Kub didn't seem to notice.

"Hey, dude? Did you hear about that boy? He's got a journal. He claims it isn't his...but any boy would when caught with their journal! Says he found it and now there's some'um about some city in the sky! *Ha*!"

I was so stunned I almost crashed our gondola. The river sprayed mist into our faces.

"Where? Where is he?"

Kub had no idea. He told me a newspaper had just published the news...and he wondered why the boy had just decided to come out with his find, instead of as soon as he found the journal. Apparently, he'd had it for some time. I thought maybe the river spray was reviving Kub from his drunken state, so I waited for more information. When there was none, I got ready to drop him off at the docks - for good that time. Just then, Kub let out a low, "OOOHHHH, baby!" I followed his eyes. I had completely forgotten about my bracelet.

We sat there in silence, watching the other. How stupid of me. I was surprised at how fast Kub was, even drunk. He snatched the bracelet off of my wrist and jumped into the water. He swam fast, too. Now I wasn't pretending. Someone had actually stolen my bracelet.

"HEY! COME BACK HERE WITH THAT! IT'S MINE!"

Kub cackled and continued swimming. Marc and Ben had heard my cry, and were paddling as fast as they could towards my gondola. I screamed at Kub again, but he was getting away. You had to remember, that was my first time every trying to steer a gondola. (I'd never even known they'd existed!)

That's when I decided my bracelet was worth it, and the gondola was not. I jumped out into the mucky river water and swam as fast as I could after Kub. I would NOT let him get away with that. That's just not the kind of person I am.

Now, do you think I got very far? No. Why, you ask? Because I didn't know how to swim. Bad idea.

The water swirled around me and my clothes dragged me down. My arms felt like weights, and I'd never used my legs for anything but walking before. Now I was kicking frantically. I couldn't believe I had let that happen. I would never get the bracelet back. It was probably a really bad idea to have taken it with me...but I never took it off, and I forgot it was even on when I left.

All of those thoughts were going through my head as I splashed through the water. I began to go under, and there was nothing I could do about it. Nothing. I was helpless...there was no escape.

"Hang on!" I heard a voice say from behind. Someone grabbed my waist and hoisted me through the water towards the dock. I struggled, thinking it was Kub, who might have somehow snuck up on me from behind, but when they dumped me onto the boardwalk I got a good look at his face. It was Marc. He'd rescued me. Actually rescued me. I hoped maybe Ben rescued my bracelet, but I later found out that hope was gone.

"You can swim?" I asked, and gagged when I felt more water in my throat.

"I've read books about it...I did my best." Marc glanced away. His wet hair fell across his forehead. I looked away, too, then pushed Marc off and got up. I walked over to Ben with whatever was left of my dignity.

Marc and I still didn't talk much, and despite the fact that I probably would've drowned if it hadn't been for him I didn't really *want* to talk.

When we got back to the inn, Marc and I cleaned off in the showers and then discussed my find over dinner.

"What now?"

"We find that newspaper," Ben replied, with a determined gleam in his eye. I smiled. That was going to be fun.

Under the cover of darkness, we slipped out of the inn and searched for a news stand. I tip-toed past building after building, shining my flashlight around to see if I could find anything. I stopped and shut the flashlight off when I heard voices.

"How stupid of that kid!" I heard the rustle of paper and then another voice. They told the first person they were surprised the parents even let the kid come out with the story. It probably wasn't even true.

I was glad people thought that. At least it wouldn't be too hard to convince them that there was no city.

When the footsteps and voices dimmed, I ran around the corner and found a newsstand. I hurriedly flipped through the paper and found a headline on the second page: 'Boy Finds Journal With Information About Ancient Civilization.' I gulped. So now they thought my city was an 'ancient civilization?' Whatever. Let them think what they wanted. I snatched the paper and met the others back at our room.

BOY FINDS JOURNAL WITH INFO ABOUT ANCIENT CIVILIZATION

The journal claims there is actually a 'City in the Sky'. It is said to be a real place, with real people and a real history. A young girl, native to this city, is said to have written a journal about her life there. Somehow, the journal has appeared here on earth, and a young boy 'just about her age' (so he says) has found it. He says that he found the journal a while ago, but thought maybe he would be reprimanded for telling lies. When his father learned about what his son had found, he read it and thought the journal quite convincing. He says he is sending up several search planes to see what they discover.

"It will be tough," he says, "Flying that high could cause some serious problems: turbulence, engine trouble...you get the drift. Anyway, I believe it's worth it." He's already sent up one plane, with no luck, but will be sending another soon.

The boy lives with his family in Rome...

The article went on to fill up the page, but I read no more. Neither did the others. We were focused on one sentence: *he will be sending up another soon*...I quickly checked the date on the newspaper and gulped. It had come out yesterday. We didn't have much time to stop the man and his son. How could we ever do it in time?

"We have to leave now! We have to go to Rome!" I cried. Marc and Ben looked at each other, then looked at me. They knew I was right. So, wordlessly, we began packing. Again.

Within minutes, we had left, with the newspaper still lying face up on the bed. One paragraph, one sentence of crucial, vital information left unread. A name...two names. The name of the son, and the name of the father.

Traveling to the Apennines

We traveled wearily all night on foot. Twice I was scared silly by a snake...but hey, you couldn't blame me! I'm only human. It was dark out and I didn't have super-night-vision like a cat. (Too bad...that would've come in handy). Venice was beautiful at night, despite the snakes and darkness. The moon shone high overhead, and the architecture of the buildings stood out in it's eerie light. The rivers glistened, and sometimes we heard the gentle singing of a gondolier.

The night wore on, and we continued to trudge on endlessly. In a matter of days we had crossed the Adige River (Venice was a little ways away from the Adige River...and we had to cross it again in order to reach the Apennines Mountains), and before we knew it we had reached the Po River, too. We stopped in Ferrara to replenish our stock of snacks and provisions, and we planned to stop in Bologna before journeying into the Apennines Mountains. Bologna was not far off of the course we'd need to take in order to reach the Arno River in the Mountains. If we found the Arno River, everything was downhill from there, because we could stop in Florence and then continue on down to Rome.

In case anyone knew the name of the girl who wrote the journal (me), we changed my name. I got to keep the same initials, for they were on my bag, and I couldn't really say the bag was not mine. It would be easier to keep my real identity a secret...safety, of course. Ben and Marc changed their names, too. I became Carina Sage, Marc was Mario, and Ben became Bernard. The names all had Italian origins, so we were set to go...although we really didn't look Italian. We had to change that, too. I was the only one who really stood out among us. Marc had dark brown hair and eyes, and Ben at least looked like some of the older men. So I pulled my light hair into a ponytail and covered it with a hat. I bought myself sunglasses and used them to cover my blue eyes. We even changed my dress, too. I hated that. I really wasn't frilly - so we had to buy me the most un-frilly outfit we could find.

It consisted of a loose, burnt orange top, and chocolate brown pants with a large belt. I bought some darker blush, too, and soon my skin looked tanner than it really was. Marc got a kick out of my new look, but something told me he was only laughing to cover up some other emotion.

Bologna really was a perfect place to stop. Newsstands were everywhere! Every time I turned the corner, we saw one. I picked one up and looked for the same headline. It wasn't the same newspaper! I rapidly flipped through, but saw nothing.

I decided to ask someone when the next paper would be out.

I saw a nice looking lady tending flower baskets on her porch. I pointed and showed Ben and Marc where I was going, then ran up to her.

"I am Carina," I stated, pointing to myself. The woman smiled.

"Me Angelina," she pointed to herself. It was going well.

"Do you know when the news next comes out?" I asked, and pointed to the newsstand. She frowned, and lowered her eyebrows. Then she shook her head.

"Io non parlo inglese e lui." She pointed first to herself, and then to her two sons I had just noticed playing up the alley. Darn. She didn't speak English. I wondered what she had said. (I later found out she had told me she didn't speak English, and neither did her two sons.)

I hurried back to Marc and Ben and we found a bench to take a quick rest. We talked about our finds (nothing) and the fact that we needed to learn Italian.

That night we left Bologna and by dawn had reached the foothills of the Apennines. Ben told us we had to be careful to make sure we were following the right river. Apparently, the Tiber River flowed from almost the same spot the Arno did, but if we followed the Tiber River, we'd end up in Rome without having stopped anywhere first. That was where we wanted to go, but who's to tell we wouldn't get lost? Even if we were following the river? No, it was better if we followed the Arno into Florence first.

We climbed FOREVER. I was so weak by the time we reached a cave at nightfall that I almost collapsed before setting up my sleeping bag. Without even saying goodnight, I crawled into it and fell fast asleep.

I woke up early; I was starting to get used to it.

We had a nice breakfast, and then Ben told us it wouldn't be far. I couldn't wait to reach the river. No more consulting the compass...wondering which way to go, if we were going the right way, if we'd ever reach our destination.

I was in the middle, trotting along behind Ben, in front of Marc, who was somewhere behind me.

Just then, I felt a tap on my shoulder. I spun around. It was only Marc, and for that I was glad. I had felt too pressured lately, too tired and confused and scared and nervous...all at once. I was ready for the whole adventure to be over...I wanted to go home, I wanted friends again, I wanted my parents and a normal life. It was something I'd felt since the whole incident, but had been trying to keep hidden deep down inside of me. If it had been some stranger behind me, trying to kidnap me or plot against me, I think I would have exploded. Screamed until my kidnapper's ears were numb.

"Hey." Marc walked up beside me. I glanced at him with the expression, 'what do you want?' I was still mad at him for 1: being an orphan, and 2: for blowing up in my face the other day when he finally did tell me he was an orphan. However, my anger was a bit dulled by his rescue. That had taken a lot of bravery and courage.

"Look...I'm sorry. For everything."

"Why didn't you tell me?" Really, that was the reason I was mad. I didn't care if he was an orphan. Was that why he didn't tell me? Because he thought I'd think he was some kind of freak?

"I...I didn't want you to feel bad for me. I didn't want you to take pity on me and treat me differently than you normally do. I didn't want our friendship to be awkward."

I thought that over for a minute. I guess it was a good argument. Even so, friends don't keep secrets...especially deep dark ones like that. I could've helped him. I wouldn't have shown him pity; I would've helped him find a nice place to live, stuff to eat.

"I could've helped."

"I didn't want you to worry about me. You had your own problems six years ago."

Six years ago! Why hadn't I paid attention to that bit of information when he told me during our fight? So that's what he meant when he had pulled out my scrapbook and said our friendship had really just begun then. Because he had come closer to me after his parents died! I was his friend, and even though I had no idea what was going on in his life, he still had someone to turn to.

"Thanks."

"No problem," He gave me a high five, then ran to catch up to Ben. I figured they were talking about that dumb cave fungus again.

A couple of hours later, I thought I heard something. A swishing...a rushing sound. "The river! We're almost there!" I cried. I was ecstatic. As long as we could reach the river safely, we could follow it to Florence. Things were definitely looking up.

"Are you sure we're hearing the river?" Marc asked skeptically.

"If it is the river, we've probably been following it for some time. We could be closer to Florence than you think! I mean, we really didn't need to follow it too far."

"I'm positive it's the river! What else could it be? A rabid bear?" I said sarcastically. I began to imitate a rabid bear - tongue hanging out of my mouth, paws up, rolling my eyes and spitting onto the rock. I probably looked really stupid. Besides, I didn't even know what a bear really even looked like! I'd only heard about them.

"Be careful, Creed!" Ben called out, but too late.

I took one step backwards and the rocks fell out from under my feet. I heard them bounce onto the ground below, but that sounded far away. Marc tried to reach out and grab me, but was too late. I wobbled once and fell.

I screamed and caught hold of the ledge I had been standing on. Marc and Ben scrambled to grab my fingers, but that only made me slip more. I shrieked again, and felt the cool air tickle my chin. I was dangling at such a dangerous height that I became dizzy, and everything around me fogged and blurred.

"Marc! Help! Heeeellllpppp!" My cries had weakened. I kicked and struggled and did the thing I had been trying so hard not to do - I looked down. It was the river alright. Bubbling and gurgling over the stones of the bank. My fingers slid over the rough ledge. I let go.

"ARRRRRRRRRGGGGGGHHHHHH!" The mountain scraped my knees and legs and shoulders as I bounced down. Bits of rock and gravel fell into my face and mouth. I was losing consciousness...all I could remember was something hitting the back of my head...and then everything going black.

♦ ♦ ♦

A Simple Question

"Should I get the door?" Mrs. Skye asked. Mr. Skye nodded, perplexed. He hadn't wanted any visitors...he had just wanted to relax, to soak in the new atmosphere. Mrs. Skye walked to the door reluctantly. She was probably thinking the same thing.

She opened the door and almost gasped aloud when she saw the person standing in the doorway. A girl, perhaps a little older than Creed, with a long gown and glittering tiara in her chocolate brown hair. Her face was drawn, tired, and in it were lines that shouldn't be there for a girl her age. Yet she was serene, graceful, and poised. The couple only knew her from public appearances and photographs - Helen, the King's youngest daughter. Katheryn was her older sister, next to ascend the throne. Many were looking forward to her rein - King Doulc was not a favorite among the people - but most forgot about Helen, waiting her turn if Katheryn should die an early death.

"I'm so sorry if I disturbed you," she said, her voice flowing into the room like honey. Her blue eyes shone, and if you weren't careful, you could probably lose yourself within them.

"No...no, not at all. Come in." Helen smiled and nodded, and swept into the room. She looked around and chose a small blue armchair to sink into. She sighed, and leaned back.

"Are you enjoying yourselves here? Do you like your quarters?"

"Yes, very much. It's...it's almost too much to grasp at one time. Why are you doing this for us?"

"It's hard to explain. I don't like to lie - and I don't want to scare you by saying this - but I think my father considers you his enemies. He thinks you knew about Creed's plan." Helen folded her hands in her lap. Mrs. Skye drew her lips into a thin line. Helen moved on quickly. "I don't agree. I think letting a child go that easily is utterly impossible unless you have a cold heart...and from all I hear, you two don't have cold hearts."

"We thought so." Mrs. Skye's voice was hardly more than a whisper, but Helen heard it nonetheless.

"I just wanted to...I came up to tell you something. My father is working on some crazy experiment which will enable him to see the World Below. I don't know how magnified it is going to be, but maybe we can pinpoint your daughter's location. I think it's possible."

"Is that the reason your father created this...came up with this experiment?"

"I'm not sure. But I also wanted to tell you that it could fall through the cracks."

"Why?"

"Because he's going to die." Mr. and Mrs. Skye gasped. How did Helen know such a thing? How old was she? 13? 14? Why was he going to die? Naturally, they began questioning her, but her face was as stony as ever. She looked distraught, and stricken with fear. All she told them was that some scientist was planning to poison him in his sleep. The same man had hidden some of the lab equipment for her father's experiment, and he didn't want to work on it anymore.

"He thinks it's too dangerous," she whispered, her eyes focused on the opposite wall. She looked lost in thought.

"Why are you telling us this?" Mr. Skye wanted to know. He looked at the teen inquisitively.

"Because I needed to know, Mr. Skye - does the poison take effect immediately?" She bit her lip and took a deep breath as she said this. She certainly was brave.

"What kind of poison is it?" Helen described the strange poison, and Mr. Skye, hating to be the bearer of bad news, paused before going on. "The poison does take effect immediately, Helen. I'm sorry."

"Don't...don't be. It's going to be alright."

"And you can't tell anybody...why, exactly...?"

"Because you cannot interfere with fate, Mrs. Skye. And because my father would not believe me."

The girl stayed for a couple of minutes longer, filling the endless time with polite conversation and banter. *Creed was exactly like this, only harsher...* Mrs. Skye couldn't help thinking. She also couldn't help thinking about how much Helen was like them. They had lost their daughter...and now Helen was going to lose her father. *Funny,* she thought.

And even after Helen had left, both only remembered her sentence: *"You cannot interfere with fate."* It was a well spoken line.

♦ ♦ ♦

The Archaeologist

"Do...do you think she's alright?"

"I don't know, Marc. Stop pestering me."

"Is anything bleeding?"

"Yes."

"Not her head...right?"

"I don't think so."

"Then she's okay? She'll recover?"

"I have no idea."

"What *is* bleeding, if it's not her head?"

"Her knees...her legs...her shoulders, arms, face...most are just minor cuts."

"How do we stop the bleeding?"

"I'm not a doctor, Marc!"

I tried to sit up, but immediately fell back down again. I was laying on something soft...cushy, and warm. I opened my eyes, but the faces before me swam and everything was blurry and fuzzy. My head was pounding, my limbs were aching, and I felt terrible. There was an awful bile taste in my mouth, and with all of the energy I could muster, I leaned over the bed and retched.

How could I continue on in such a state?

I leaned back onto my bed and closed my eyes again. I took a short nap before I had enough energy to open them.

Towering over me sat Marc and Ben. Ben was in the process of tying a bandage around my arm, and Marc was staring down at me anxiously.

"Where am I?" I whispered.

"We found a cave just off the river," Marc whispered back. "Then we wrapped you up in the sleeping bags and Ben started to take care of your wounds."

"Thanks." This time, I only smiled, and saved my energy. I had a feeling I'd be needing it.

Ben was done in a second, and then he pulled Marc away from where I lay. They whispered there together for a couple of minutes before they came back. They'd glance over at me, then point in the opposite direction and whisper all over again. It was annoying, and making me dizzy.

They were back soon, and Ben pushed the hair out of my eyes. He said gently,

"I'm sorry, Creed, but we have to leave you here for now. You're bleeding too much and I have no idea how to stop some of the larger cuts. We'll have to find a doctor. Be good, alright?"

"No!" Marc cried, and leaned over me protectively. "What if something happens again? She's too weak to stay here all by herself!"

"And neither you nor I can go into that city alone. I think she'll be fine. Let's go." Marc glanced at me one last time before reluctantly following Ben out of the cave.

Why did they want to do that? I understood I needed a doctor...but why leave me there to suffer and possibly die? I took a deep breath and laughed. What I really needed was to get my bearings...I wasn't going to die! I could take care of myself. With those thoughts in my head, I continued to take deep breaths and eventually fell asleep.

◆ ◆ ◆

Ben, followed by Marc, marched out of the cave. Marc looked back at Creed. How serene and peaceful she looked; yet beat up and in pain. Marc desperately hoped she'd fall back asleep, for she constantly needed company and didn't like being alone. Maybe if she slept through his and Ben's absence, the time would pass quicker for her.

He sighed, then caught back up to Ben. The two walked in silence for some time, then Marc asked,

"Do you really think she'll be alright? That's my last question." Ben looked down at his feet, then spoke,

"I hope so. As long as we can find someone, anyone, I think they will be able to help her."

For another couple of hours the pair walked and walked, up and down mountain peaks and trails and around bends and hills. They had left the river behind to cut into Florence.

At last, the edge of the city came into view. Ben and Marc broke into a run. If they didn't find someone fast, Creed could lose a lot of blood. They began searching random streets, running up and down and pulling on the sleeves of whoever they met. However, they came across the same problem almost every time: No one spoke English.

"Creed had the same problem, you know. In Bologna. The woman said something like: 'Io no parlor inglese luigi.'"

"Grrr...we have to get back to Creed. If only we could find *someone!*" Ben scanned the area once more, then spotted a lone tourist taking pictures of the mountains. "I bet you he doesn't speak Italian!"

They ran over to the man as fast as their legs would carry them.

"Ex...cuse me...but...we need...a doctor," Marc panted.

"Ciao!" The tourist cried, and broke into a large grin.

"Ciao," Marc replied grudgingly, then said, "Arrivederci." Those were the only two Italian words he knew. They meant 'hello' and 'goodbye'.

"Wait!" The tourist cried out as they turned away. "Do you speak English?" Marc whirled around.

"Duh! We thought for a minute you spoke Italian!" The man laughed.

"Nope! Only those two words." Marc smiled. He liked the man at once. Ben put his hands on Marc's shoulders and explained,

"Sir, we need a doctor. My daughter took a nasty fall off of one of those mountains and now she's in bad shape. We need a doctor right away. I know you must not know too much about the medical field here...but if you do know anything...we'd really love to know." Ben and Marc waited pleadingly for the tourist. Slowly, he said,

"I think I can help. I just visited a rather interesting presentation about remedies used for medical needs. The man travels Italy to find the remedies, and the presentation was very intriguing. He'll probably know what to do. I'll take you to him at once."

"Thank you!" Marc let out a pent up breath. The three began walking farther into the city.

Marc wondered who the man could be, but it didn't really matter. As long as he knew remedies that would help Creed, they'd take him. Marc hoped he was available.

The tourist, who's name was Kyle, continued snapping pictures on the way there.

"It was a large tent set up in the middle of a beautiful courtyard...I made sure to take lots of pictures...ah, there it is! You wait here!" Kyle sprinted into the tent, and Marc and Ben took a seat on a bench in the courtyard. They waited and tried to make out voices in the tent. They wondered if the man had begun another presentation. Just then, there was a rustle behind the tent's flap. Out walked Kyle and a tall, handsome man dressed for a formal presentation.

"Marc! Ben! What a surprise!" The archaeologist. Griffin was in Florence.

"How did you get here?" Marc asked on their way into Griffin's tent. He needed to get his medical bag before they ran back to Creed.

"I'll tell you later. First, Marc, I need you to get that black bag over there. It's my luggage. There's a first aid kit in it and I have my bag of remedies. It's over here." Ben hovered over Griffin as he bent down to get his medical bag. It didn't look like a medical bag at all. Inside were a bunch of spiky plants, jars of honey, cabbage leaves, garlic, and more. Instead, it looked like a bag of tricks.

"Is this some kind of joke?" Ben asked.

"Are you kidding? No way! I don't have time to explain now, but I'll tell you everything when we get to Creed's cave."

They left a minute later, and after running halfway there, slowed to a jog. Ben and Marc wanted explanations, but there had been no time to talk as the mountains zipped past. With every extra second they took, Creed was losing blood.

The wind was on their side, and it seemed to be pushing them in the right direction. With every breath they took, it filled their lungs and made them strong again. The bitter cold of the mountain air kept them fresh and exuberant. The grass swayed when they ran past. The sun was sinking lower and lower in the sky. Marc and Ben were worried.

They'd been gone for so long that they hadn't even had lunch. What if Creed had awoken and wanted food...only to find she didn't have enough energy to get any?

Marc's stomach was doing back flips, but he continued running anyway. They had to get back to Creed.

♦ ♦ ♦

Healing

I awoke to find three faces staring over me. Marc, Ben, and Griffin. Griffin? Was I dreaming? Was I delusional? How did he get there?

"Am I seeing things?" I asked quietly. Marc laughed.

"Nope! Creed, it's Griffin. Can you believe it? He was giving a presentation in Florence on his remedies and he agreed to come help you!"

"Yes, I did. Trouble seems to find you, doesn't it Creed?"

"You have *no* idea," I whispered. Griffin ordered Ben and Marc to get him his bags, then began to heal my wounds. He told us each and every one of his remedies.

"Honey will help stop the bleeding. These spiky plants are aloe, and if you cut off the tip, you can squeeze the medicine out. It stops cuts and scratches from burning. Cabbage helps heal cuts and wounds, and so does garlic. I want you to eat those. Get them down with a water bottle. After I apply the remedies, I can use my first aid kit to bandage you up. The cuts and scrapes should heal in no time, but you're going to be sore for a little while. Now about all of those large gashes. We're going to have to apply the remedies and then put some gauze on them and wrap them up. A make-shift cast kind of thing. Did you break any bones?"

"I have no idea. I don't think so. I know I hit my head."

Marc and Ben laughed. Then Ben explained,

"Creed, you fell into the river. What you felt before going unconscious was your body coming in contact with the water."

I tried to sort everything out...how badly I was hurt, how long it would take to heal, the job of every remedy...it seemed like too much. I wanted to go back to sleep again, but I knew it would be easier for Griffin if I was able to tell him where everything hurt.

To clean the cuts out, Griffin had Ben bring him a water bottle. After sliding me onto the cold cave floor, he poured the water onto my various cuts, scrapes, and gashes. He said it should clean them out, but the sensation was terrible! Every single cut stung like the dickens! It felt as if fire was spreading through my body, tickling every wound I'd ever had. Griffin apologized for the pain, but I couldn't forgive him yet. I hurt too much. He dabbed at the wounds and cleaned them of the dirt, dust, and gravel. Tears filled my eyes as he did so. Finally, he was satisfied, and he made sure the water was gone so he could begin his remedies.

The honey came first. He dabbed some of the sticky stuff on the cuts still seeping blood. It felt really weird...cold and sticky and moist. He rubbed the substance into the wounds and it didn't burn as much as I had expected. When he was done with the honey, he opened his first-aid kit and took out some white gauze, tape, and an ace bandage. He taped the gauze onto the cuts he'd just rubbed the honey onto, and then took the ace bandage and wound it around my ankle, which now had a lump-sized bruise. It would be hard to walk.

Now that the gashes had been taken care of, it was time for my burning cuts and scrapes. He took out some of the spiky plants and ripped off their spiky tops. He let us all take a peek into the plant. Some gooey substance was inside! He squeezed the plant gently, and the gooey stuff oozed to the top. He put some on his finger and rubbed the aloe onto my cuts and scrapes. It was cold...but the burning was thankfully subsiding. He covered the larger ones with small band aids, but the ones that were already healing he left alone. He rubbed me down with some lotion to soothe me, and got me some clothes to change into. Griffin, Ben, and Marc went outside to talk, and I held up a sleeping bag in front of me while I changed.

When I was done, they came back in and Griffin ordered me to lay down and rest.

"I've decided to accompany you," he announced, then hastily added, "If you guys would like me to."

"We'd love you to!" Ben commented. "I think Creed is going to be needing your help for a while."

"Well, I have my very own caravan, and we can travel in that. Where did you guys want to go next?"

"ROME!" I screamed. If Griffin wasn't going there, and didn't agree to go there, I was NOT traveling with him. I had to get that journal...I had to save my city. I wasn't about to let some archaeologist change my plans.

"Perfect. I was heading there myself. Time to go back home." I relaxed. It would really work out after all. "I'd better go and get the caravan. It's back at the tent. You guys stay here and take care of Creed. She should be fine while I'm gone, although she may be really sore...not to mention tired. Watch her closely," With that, Griffin smiled and ran off into the dusk.

I did what he said and rested, while Ben and Marc barely even blinked while watching me. I think they took Griffin's comment a little too literally.

Finally, Griffin returned. His caravan was rumbling so loudly I could hear it a mile away. He cut the engine as he pulled up in front of the cave. He laughed as he got out. "Bumpy ride!"

We loaded up as quickly as possible. It was time to hit the road. Because of my injuries, my job was to roll up the sleeping bags. Marc got all of the bags, and Ben went into the caravan to inspect it and to make sleeping arrangements.

We were ready to go in ten minutes flat. Ben held my hand as I stepped into the caravan. It was very spacey, and already there were bunk beds pulled down on each side. Griffin was at the wheel, and Ben sat down in the seat beside him.

"I've decided that you and Marc will share a bunk bed, and Griffin and I will share the other." Ben explained. He told us that Marc should sleep on the top, and me on the bottom. Our packs had been set in our beds, and I hurried over to my bunk.

With a sigh, I plopped down into it. It was very comfy; I had forgotten how good a bed could feel when you're really tired. I looked around. I was pretty much closed in. The bunk bed extended from the wall into a small cove, so there was a wall on three sides. The ladder covered half of the space to get out. I was glad it was that way. I was used to sleeping in private, where if I mumbled in my sleep or snored or drooled nobody would know. I was a little uneasy sleeping with people so close. I had been trying to forget about it, but the bunk bed came as a great relief. I crawled under the covers and took joy in the fact that I had a real pillow to sleep on! Just then, I noticed something about my bed that I hadn't seen before. There were blinds on the wall! There had to be a window.

Quick as a flash, I pulled down the blinds. Yes! There was a window! The engine of the caravan sputtered to life, and we began rumbling down the road. I relaxed and watched out the glass as we passed the mountains, river, caves, and underbrush. I saw many a bird cawing for a friend, and I saw little creatures diving in and out of the leaves of trees and bushes. The sky ahead was getting darker and darker as night fell. I got sleepier and sleepier. I fought to keep my eyelids open, to continue watching the outdoors, but I couldn't. I was too weak. In a matter of minutes, I had fallen fast asleep under the comfy covers of the caravan's bunk bed.

Hours later, my eyes blinked open to bright light streaming through the blinds. Darn! I had forgotten to close them when I went to sleep! The thing was, if I had been so tired, why had only light awakened me? I could hear voices. Had those cut into my dreams as well? Nah. My dad had said so. I sleep like a log. But then I noticed something...we weren't moving. I sat up with a jolt...and conked my head on the bed above.

"OUCH!" I already had enough injuries; why did I need one more?

"Creed?" I held my breath. Who was that? "Creed?" I sighed. It was just Marc in his bed above me.

"Yeah? I'm awake," I answered him.

"Really? Get up here." I wondered why Marc needed me to go see him. But it must have been important, so I climbed out of bed and up the ladder. I settled in beside him.

"What's up?" I asked groggily.

"Engine trouble. Flat tire," he answered. We sat there for a moment, letting the words sink in. Engine trouble? A flat tire? How could that be? We had to get to Rome! And quick! We still had a long way to go.

I jumped up and hurried back down to my bunk. Then I ran outside into the morning air. I followed the caravan towards the voices, and when I heard them, I didn't go any further. I peeked around the corner. There they were - Ben and Griffin. They were having a heated discussion. I listened closely.

"I'm sorry, Ben! But there's nothing we can do about this! Yes, I know I should have been smart enough to make sure I had a spare tire before we left, but now it's out of our hands! I want to get back too!"

"Griffin. Listen close. It's not that I *want* to get to Rome quickly...but I *need* to get to Rome quickly."

Had Ben told Griffin our secret? Why was he giving us away?

"Really? We could all argue that, Ben."

"No, Griffin. Have you *seen* Creed? She is in terrible shape...and even with your remedies, I'm really worried about her. We need to get her to a doctor. A real doctor. She can barely even get out of bed without taking a nap to save energy first. If we're going to be travelers, she needs as much energy as she can get. I mean, what happens when we get to Rome and we can't travel in your caravan anymore?"

Griffin's voice softened. "I know you're concerned, Ben, but I'm sure regular doctors would have done exactly the same thing. Sure, they could have given her some medicine or something...but either way, however it was done, they would have had to clean the wounds first, dress them, and then tell you she would take some time to heal. Now, as for Rome, I'm doing my best. I promise you...we'll think of something. Let's inspect that tire."

I tiptoed back inside the caravan and crawled up to Marc's bunk, where he was reading the book on the World Below. He put the book down as soon as I got there.

"What are they fighting about? I heard Ben tell Griffin we needed to get to Rome...but why? He didn't...right?"

"No. He didn't tell. He just told Griffin he was really worried about me and needed to get me to a real doctor."

"Ahhhh." We sat in thought for a moment. Then, out of nowhere, Marc smiled and said, "Let's go exploring!"

"WHAT?" I stared at him in shock. "You know I can't go exploring! I can barely get out of bed! What are you thinking?"

"I was thinking I'd go alone."

I narrowed my eyes. "Oh. So you said 'let's' but you really mean 'I'. I get it. You did that on purpose."

"Exactly." Marc hopped out of bed and handed me the book on his way out the door. "See yah. I'm bored."

I groaned, but crawled back down to my bunk to read anyway.

◆ ◆ ◆

Secrets

Marc tried to contain his smile as he skipped away from the bunks and out the door. He told Ben where he was going, and then ran. He had to get away. He'd hardly been alone since they started the journey, and he was tired of listening to Creed every second of the day. Even Ben. He had to admit...when Ben started ranting on and on about cave fungus, the weird kind, he got really tired. He only liked the specific kind he'd read about in the book. Marc had grown fond of that book. It was so interesting, and he'd learned a lot. He'd always been a smart kid, despite the fact that it was hard to pay for schooling.

He wasn't normally in school for the normal hours. He'd told Creed he was...different. He didn't want to say 'smarter' but she already knew. She seemed to know everything about him. The teacher knew, too, and had immediately decided to take him in and house and shelter him. Marc made sure she never said anything to any of his friends...or his friend's parents. It was easy, because she decided to give him tutoring in the mornings, and at times when the other kids were only doing classwork or playing outside. This was mainly because he already understood everything the kids were learning. He could be learning new things during those times, and staying in school for the normal hours listening to things he already knew was boring, and it was holding him back.

Marc payed his 'mother' back by being a good kid. He never complained, did what he was told, and was sweet and understanding. Ms. Blue loved him. Marc also made sure not to let Creed see him and Ms. Blue together except for tutoring times. He'd told Ms. Blue all about Creed and the reasons he didn't want her to know he was an orphan, so she'd never show him special attention around her. It was pretty much an easy life. Super easy. But sad, and lonely, too. Only Creed made him feel normal again.

Marc had felt extremely terrible when he told her. She'd been so upset...and he didn't know what to say or do to comfort her. He rarely felt like that. Normally he knew everything about her...the way she was feeling, why she felt that way, what to say to help her...but when he'd revealed his secret, she'd gone nuts and he'd gone haywire. Neither knew how to fix it.

Now Marc stuck his hands in his pockets and sighed. When he got back he'd have to tell Creed about his life...his real life. The life he'd lived behind a closed door from her. The secret life.

He smiled. Only a small part of him was proud of what he'd done. He'd kept a secret from Creed! Nosy, stubborn, dignified Creed. It made him want to laugh. He did.

Marc glanced up at the sky and frowned. It looked as if it would rain later. He hoped not. It was already so cold in Italy; he didn't think he could stand another drop in temperature. But hey...he had to endure what he had to endure. He had to stay strong. That was another thing that made the journey so hard: staying strong in front of Creed. So many times already he'd felt the need to give up and go home. Even thinking about Creed's journal and the life of denial she'd lived barely drove him on anymore.

He kicked around a small pebble for a while, enjoying the way it bounced over the rocky terrain. They had only reached the tip of the Arno River, the edge of the Apennines, the border of the rolling hills yet to come. He knew in his heart they probably wouldn't make it. But how to explain that to Creed?

Up ahead he neared a jagged piece of jutting rock. He climbed up to it and sat on the edge, letting his legs dangle over the side. He peered down at the bushes. Something was sticking out of one of them, waving in the breeze. A branch from the bush was pinning it down.

Marc hopped off his ledge and approached the bush cautiously. He stared at the bush, surprised. The thing stuck in the leaves and sticks of the bush was a piece of paper! He plucked it from the branch and smoothed it against his jeans. Then he looked at it searchingly.

He couldn't believe what he saw. Creed's handwriting covered the front and back. The cramped letters filled the page. The passage was dated six years ago. He sucked in his breath and let out a whoop. Creed's journal was definitely in Italy! The page must have come out of the book and floated into the bush.

Marc whooped again and raced back to camp, eager to share his find with Creed.

◆ ◆ ◆

The couple of chapters I read in Marc's book were immensely interesting. I read all about the peoples of the world, the languages they spoke, their religions, history, and more. I was amazed. I read about the governments and exports and imports and crops grown. It really intrigued me to know that such a big place could run so smoothly. I realized there was much to learn, and I couldn't wait to learn it. For a minute, I sat there and laughed out loud. What I was feeling was probably what Marc felt all the time.

Time passed so quickly I couldn't even believe it. When Marc returned, I even asked him why he'd only stayed out for a couple of minutes. He looked at me strangely, then started talking and panting so quickly I couldn't understand a word.

"In English, please," I asked. He rolled his eyes and handed me a piece of paper.

"Read," he instructed, then smiled broadly.

...Anyway, I felt Ms. Blue was being extremely unfair. Why else would she not have let me pass to the third level of spelling words? I know how to spell 'gipsy'! Whatever. I'll have Marc help me. He's an academic whiz.

Amy told me it was probably because Ms. Blue thinks I'm spoiled. I took this to mean that Amy probably thinks I'm spoiled, too, but I let it go. I asked her, "Why on earth would I seem spoiled?" She just pointed to my neatly pulled back hair, my pressed uniform, my gold bracelet, and my expensive lunch box. I just rolled my eyes and calmly explained to her that I was 'well taken care of' and not 'spoiled.' Have you looked up the word 'spoil' in the dictionary before? It means: 'to cause to expect too much by overindulgence.' I am not overindulged. Okay, okay...the gold bracelet may cause someone to think I'm overindulged, but it was a present when I was a baby. Mom and Dad gave it to me. My name is engraved on the back, and I've never, ever taken it off. I love it. It is a priceless treasure. Every time I say this, though, they tell me, "YOU are the priceless treasure. Sometimes...I wish there were two of you."

Ahhhhhh...here comes Marc.

I just asked him how to spell 'gipsy.' He says it's: 'g-y-p-s-y.' No one is on my side today! Well, it's time to go play. I'll see you next time ON...just kidding. I love my journal! (I know that's really random)

I laughed as soon as I was done reading the entry. I must have been a riot as a seven year old. Obviously, I was a bit vain.

"Am...am I still that way?"

"Not really...only sometimes," Marc teased.

"This is...is...awesome! I can't believe you found it!" Marc told me how he'd found the journal page, then added,

"I want to tell you something. I thought about it, and I think you're ready. I should have told you before, but I think we were both too wound up." I wondered what he was talking about. When he began, though, I soon remembered. "I've been living with Ms. Blue all of these years. She's been my guardian, not just my tutor. She's provided me with food, shelter, and love."

"I was wondering about that," I whispered. We looked away from each other. Marc's life was becoming a touchy subject, although I thought we were getting better. I hoped so. Never before had we felt that way when discussing something.

"...Yes, yes...we'll think of something." We whipped around. Ben and Griffin were coming into the caravan. Luckily, my pack was right next to me, and I stuffed the entry into it.

"We're sorry, kids, but we'll have to camp here for the night. Creed, how are you feeling?"

"I'm doing fine. Sore, and tired like you said - but I'm fine nevertheless."

"Such a trooper." Ben came over and sat down next to me. He had taken the 'father' role for Marc and I. It felt good, considering I was miles and miles and miles and miles away from my real father.

The night went by quickly. I watched and relaxed as the sun went down, and then watched some more as the first stars popped into the sky. It was so beautiful. I made a note to observe the stars once I got back to Pastel. It was a class in high school.

Daylight appeared, and I woke up with a start. I was sweating. I wondered if I'd gotten hot during the night, or, worse, if I'd just broken a fever.

Once again, Ben and Griffin were outside, and Marc was in his bunk reading. I climbed up to join him. I peeked over his shoulder and read the passage. Luckily, it wasn't one on cave fungus.

It was lunch time when we received the call. It came on Griffin's cell phone, and he practically dropped it in his haste to answer it.

"Hello?" he asked eagerly. He relaxed when he heard the voice on the other end of the line. "Cameron!...no...we're nowhere near...we're a bit stuck. We've got a flat tire and engine trouble. No, I mean, we can't find one...yes, yes, I know...any suggestions?...Perfect! Cameron, you're a genius!...love you too...bye...wait! Call me back soon..."

Griffin didn't even have time to answer our questions before he was out the door and bustling around outside. About a minute later, we heard a loud: "YES!" and then, "*NICE*, CAMERON!" I wondered what Cameron could've suggested. Ben was on his way outside to see what Griffin was so excited about when Griffin himself bounded back into the caravan.

"Good news!" he cried. "Cameron reminded me that there's at least a tire pump in all rental cars. As long as we can find it, we're set to go!"

"Sweet!" I tried to jump up and down, but failed miserably. Bursts of pain shot through my legs and back. "OUCH!" I screamed.

"CREED! You're not supposed to do that!" Marc rushed over to me and helped me get back into bed. I humphed. It wasn't fair. Life wasn't fair. But at least we'd make it to Rome after all! Whether we got there in time or not, we'd at least get there safe and sound. (I hoped.)

◆ ◆ ◆

The Reveal, The Poison, and A Death

Another two weeks had gone by. King Doulc was sitting on his throne once again, grumpy because it was past lunch time and Helen had still not come with her report. She showed up later and later every day. What was he to do with her? Replace her with another spy? No, she was perfect. She had just the right amount of authority, and she was definitely inconspicuous. She'd probably never become Queen - so people didn't really notice her.

The King was beginning to have Deja Vu. There came the boring entertainers, the servants in the doorway, and Twitter scuttling about on his twig legs.

"Your highness! Your majesty! I have a message from Princess Helen for you!"

"It's about time!" Doulc roared, and jumped off the throne. He held out his hand and waited.

"Ummm...it's not a written message, sir. Helen said it could be intercepted too easily. She trusts me, so she told me to tell you." He looked proud of himself for being trusted, but his silly grin was wiped away only too quickly.

"Then what is it, Twitter?"

"She wants to see you." King Doulc could've pulled his hair out he was so frustrated. She wanted to see him? So that was the message? She sent Twitter all the way from the depths of the lab to the throne room to tell him that she wanted to *see him*? If she wanted to see him so badly, she should have done so at LUNCH TIME!

"Send for her. I cannot climb down those stairs again. I'll kill myself." With a sigh, King Doulc plopped back onto his throne, sending his crown bouncing to the floor. Before Twitter had a chance to pick it up, someone else did. Someone with slender wrists and fragile hands. Helen.

"I'm sorry I could not come sooner, father. I was learning some interesting news. You have to forgive me." Sometimes, it was hard to remember that Helen was only 14. She was not your average teen. She placed the crown back onto her father's head and pressed a silver dollar coin into Twitter's palm. He raced away happily.

"What is this news? Is it something I'll like? Has more material been stolen?" Doulc had replaced the stolen items, of course, but things seemed to disappear more rapidly than he could make them reappear.

"Nothing else has been stolen, yet, but the scientists have decided they are half way done and would like to show you their progress. They told me to tell you that they would hold a presentation tomorrow at noon."

"For me? How kind! But I'd better like this progress, Helen, or someone is going to be fired. Most likely Mack. He's the one overseeing the project."

A hint of fear danced in Helen's eyes as she assured her father that the project was coming along nicely. "Really, father! You'll be very pleased." Before walking away, she took his hand and kissed his forehead. She looked almost sad as she did so, but tried to hide it by smiling broadly. "I'll go tell Katheryn! She won't want to miss it."

But King Doulc did not ever get to see the presentation. That night, as he was slipping into his sleep wear, he turned to find an intruder standing by his bedside, holding a poisoned dart in hand. He grabbed a piece of paper from his bedside table and scribbled a message quickly. It dropped to the floor when the man advanced. All he could remember before dying was a sharp pain in his neck, a cackle, his scream, and darkness. Eternal darkness.

The two daughters held each other in their arms. Katheryn wept, and Helen was filled with grief. They rocked back and forth together in their room, trying to remember his presence and the good things about him. It was pretty hard, but Doulc was still their father, and losing a father is a hard thing to have happen to you. It shatters your heart into a million pieces, pieces impossible to fully repair again.

Yet grief was not the only thing filling the castle next day. There were preparations to make...invitations to send out. There was a coronation to plan, a funeral to host. Doulc was dead, and the next royal family member in line was Katheryn. She would become queen in a week, no more no less.

Helen went to visit Mr. and Mrs. Skye, for they were the only ones who knew what she did, and they tried to comfort her. But she was not one who needed to be comforted.

"We're so sorry. So sorry. We know you loved your father."

"It had to happen sometime. It was for the best. I'm sure Katheryn will make a great Queen." Helen replied wearily. Nonetheless, a tear rolled down her cheek and she let Mrs. Skye wrap her arms around her.

Even though Katheryn had not been officially crowned, she was still pretty much the Queen. Her first announcement was to continue on with the presentation that her father had wanted to see so badly. She decided that it was better to see what had been accomplished, and then continue on from there. If the scientists were not almost finished, she would call off the project and send the scientists home. If there was a chance of finishing, she would provide the necessary materials and let the scientists continue.

She was able to weed out the scientist who had poisoned her father with the help of Helen, and together they decided to throw him in jail. It was a pretty bad thing to kill a King, and demanded serious consequences. Besides, the man must have had at least some mental issues. Even the other scientists in the lab admitted he had not been much help.

At noon that day, Katheryn called for the King's old advisors and Helen to sit in on the presentation. Not all of the scientists came. Only the lead scientists were present, and on a cart they pulled in the device.

It was very large. It barely fit through the door, but after turning the cart several different ways they were able to fit it into the room. It was covered in a white sheet, and when they removed it, there were several gasps of delight. The telescope was gigantic, with a very wide, thick lens in front. It wasn't finished, but it looked very close. Mack explained that they needed to magnify the lens more, and thin it out so it would be easier to look through. Accompanying the project was a small dry erase board on which Mack and the others explained how the telescope worked.

Like most telescopes, of course. However, this one was highly magnified and could see up to 5,000 miles away. The knob on the side changed the magnification. It had to be handled gently because it was a very fragile thing, and at that particular time only the top scientists and Queen Katheryn were allowed to touch it.

The advisors took notes the entire time, and Katheryn made sure to ask plenty of questions. She wanted to understand exactly how it worked.

"Tell me - where do you plan to put this?"

"We were going to ask you the same thing."

"What do you suggest, for something like that?"

"Not a place where normal people can get their hands on it. I suggest somewhere on the castle grounds so that only the royals and those specialized can touch it. It was invented for the King, you know. And now it is for our Queen."

Katheryn gave Mack her best smile. That was what you had to do when you became Queen. You couldn't show your real emotions; they were your weakness. Only those close to you could be told. Helen, for instance, saw right through Katheryn's smile. Poor Katheryn was weary and hungry.

"Thank you for this, Mack, but we have to go now. It is Katheryn's first lunch as Queen."

Mack nodded in acknowledgement. "We will be on our way now, Queen Katheryn."

"We thank you very much. Keep up the good work and I will continue to send my sister down to see you and check on your progress." With that, the scientists rolled the cart out of the room and went back down to the lab.

"Come on, Ryn, let's go have some lunch." Helen grabbed her sister's arm and they headed out the back door.

◆ ◆ ◆

Rome

I was so relieved Ben and Griffin had gotten the caravan back on the road that I almost broke out in song. But then I remembered that life wasn't a musical. Too bad.

Sometime before lunch the next day, we stopped in Siena. It was a beautiful little city, and we enjoyed having lunch there. I think everyone was getting annoyed with me, though, for every five minutes I had to rest. Probably more worried than annoyed...especially in Ben and Marc's cases.

LL Capriccio was a wonderful spot for our lunch. We ordered one giant cheese/pepperoni pizza and it was literally the best I've ever eaten. The service was splendid and the spot was crowded with locals. A couple of times we were asked if we were tourists, and all of us except Griffin answered 'yes.' Was it really that obvious?

We were back on the road a couple of hours later. The city was marvelous and quaint, but we had to stick to a schedule. Griffin seemed really eager to get back to his family. I felt bad for the guy...but couldn't help thinking about our predicament. Ben probably hadn't seen his family in years, Marc had no family except his 'mother' the schoolteacher, and I'd never been away from my parents for more than one night when on sleepovers. I wondered what my parents were doing at that very moment.

Once we were comfortably settled on Marc's bunk, he read a passage from his book aloud to me:

Rome

Rome is a city like no other. A place of art, history, and beauty, Rome is breathtaking and intriguing. Rome was the home of many fabulous artists, and is the home of famous museums, churches, ancient ruins, fountains, statues, and monuments today. Rome is said to have been started by Romulus and Remus - two boys who were raised by a wolf.

Vatican City lies within Rome - and is the home of the Roman Catholic Church Pope. He lives in the Vatican. There are beautiful museums and churches in Vatican City, and it is known as the 'smallest independent state in the world.'

There are some really wonderful monuments and buildings in Rome, including the Spanish Steps, the Colosseum, the Vatican, the Sistine Chapel, and more. At the bottom of the Spanish Steps is a fountain shaped like a boat. The Colosseum was the largest outdoor theater in the whole city, and was four stories tall. The Sistine Chapel has paintings from the Bible on it's ceiling, painted by Michelangelo.

Famous foods in Italy can be found all over...even in Rome. When in Rome...be sure to try the different pastas, pizzas, and gelato. A few Italian words are as follows...

"Hey! Look at this one! 'Pastello.' It means crayon. If only it meant *Pastel!* You have to admit, they're pretty close. Then we'd have learned the name of our city in Italian!"

"Cool!" I said. We smiled at each other for a moment. Marc put the book down when Ben came leaping into the caravan.

"Oh, kids! We're on the road again! To Rome..."

"And BEYOND!" We screamed. Griffin may have had no idea what that meant, but we did. *Beyond* meant back to Pastel. How we would get back was a different story...

On the way there, I begged Griffin to tell me more about Cameron. I bet the kid didn't even speak English, but I wanted to be polite. I probably wouldn't even meet him anyway. Once we got to Rome, we'd go our separate ways.

"For instance...why is his name Cameron? Aren't you guys Italian?"

"Yes, indeed we are. Andria's mother was English, however, and her uncle's name was Cameron. So we picked the name Cameron. Andria's pregnant, again, though, and we're going to name the new baby - a boy - an Italian name. Possibly Rocco. But Cameron...Cameron...how to describe Cameron...well, for one thing, he's extremely smart." Marc rolled his eyes. I copied. "He speaks four different languages, not counting Italian: English, Portuguese, French, and Spanish. He is in all honors classes and scores way above the other kids in his testing. He's already studying to become an archaeologist like me, and a doctor. I just know he's going to be very successful."

My eyes nearly popped out of my head. My jaw dropped open. Marc was stunned. The kid could speak 5 different languages? He was already studying to be an archaeologist *and* a doctor? Who *was* this guy? I was actually relieved that I wasn't going to have to really meet him. Despite our emotions, Griffin continued.

"Cameron is really good natured, too. Also kind and loving and understanding. He's very literal. He has a wonderful personality...I wish you guys could meet him. He'd love to meet you. In fact, I know he wants to meet you. He's very curious."

Curious about what? I wanted to ask, but held my tongue. I think Marc was thinking the same thing.

Luckily, I fell asleep during the rest of Griffin's speech. I shouldn't even have asked about his Super Man son. Too much information. The truth was, deep down inside...I think I may have been jealous. Marc, too.

We continued to travel for what seemed like days. There were no more cities to stop in that were in our path. We traveled day and night, because Ben and Griffin took turns. Luckily, Griffin had a map, and Ben was able to follow that. Vatican City was approaching quickly. Because Griffin lived somewhere near the Trevi Fountain, he said he would drop us off there.

I was quite excited about nearing Rome. It meant stopping the father and son who were sending up the plane...it meant getting my journal back...I couldn't wait. The only trouble was this: I was not in good health.

Griffin said we had about three hours left to travel. I was squealing with delight when Ben took the wheel. Griffin conked out and we were free to talk.

"I can't believe it! We might actually make it!" I bounced up and down in the bunk, and Marc gave me a warning glance. I stopped before I hurt myself.

"Creed, don't count on it. Our time is up. There must have been some technical difficulties with the plane...but I'm sure they'll be fixed soon."

It hadn't even been five minutes later when Marc shook me so hard I almost toppled out of the bunk.

"Do you hear that?" he hissed. I shook my head. What was he talking about? He yanked on the blinds and we peered out the window. I heard it then. A slow rumbling sound...coming nearer and nearer...and then it appeared over the top of a mountain in the distance. A plane. Sleek and slender, shining in the moonlight, the plane was fast and deliberate. It was ascending with tremendous speed, higher and higher until it disappeared among the clouds. That was it. We had failed. Everything we had come Below for, all of the hopes I had been sheltering for so long...all of it was gone. A tear rolled down my cheek. I pressed my face into my pillow and sobbed. I had failed. Failed...failed...failed...it was an ugly word.

I think I passed out after my eyes couldn't cry anymore. They were swollen shut and red and my face was blotchy. I wanted to cry more, but nothing would come out.

Over the next two hours, Ben just continued to tell Griffin that I wasn't feeling good, that I had fallen ill again. Had a relapse. Griffin believed it, and so did I...for the most part.

When we reached Vatican City I couldn't even look out the window. I refused to talk, to get up, to do anything but bury myself down under my pillow and covers. I wanted to disappear...to evaporate, like I had watched clouds do back at Pastel. Pastel. I had failed them, too. My whole city was probably under siege at that very moment. That made me cry even more.

I missed the entire conversation Griffin had with Ben. Griffin flatly refused to leave me. He argued with Ben that he knew of every doctor and hospital in the city, and he should house us while I was still under recovery. I knew I'd never recover...but I didn't mention that to Griffin. I wasn't speaking.

I think I was napping when they lifted me out of the caravan and into Griffin's house, when they pried my mouth open to make me take medicine, when Griffin introduced

Ben and Marc to Andria and Cameron, and when Griffin called a doctor to come and see my condition. I really did sleep through it all. The only thing I can remember is when I opened my eyes for the first time after being in Rome. I was in a bed, a real bed, in someone's house. The walls were white, the sheets were white, the blinds were open and white light was pouring across my face. I yawned and stretched and realized I was wearing a nightgown...white, of course. Everything felt like a dream. I tiptoed silently out of bed and peered down the hall, half expecting God to appear from out of one of the doors. He didn't. Instead, I followed the sound of voices.

They were coming from many different rooms. I could hear Marc's voice and another voice inside one of the rooms. Ben's voice and Griffin's were floating through the door of another. I didn't go in either. I wanted to investigate the house first. As if in a dream, I walked quietly down the hallway and past the two doors. I passed the living room, very attractive at that, and into the kitchen. I stopped short when I saw the back of a middle aged woman. Before I had time to back out, she turned around and saw me.

"Creed!" She cried in a heavy Italian accent. Her tummy was huge. I suspected that was Rocco. Surprisingly, she didn't look as Italian as I thought she would. She had long, wavy brown hair, and a big smile. Her eyes were big and milky. Andria opened her arms and held me in a tight embrace before holding me out at arms' length. "You look much better." She commented. "Let's get you some clothes to change into."

She led me back down the hall and back into the room I had been lying in. I spotted my pack hanging on a small hook, and sighed with relief. Andria opened the closet doors to reveal a neatly organized wardrobe.

"I managed to find some clothes from friends that I think will fit you. Here, try this on." She handed me a pale yellow sun dress and some sandals.

I slipped it on and examined myself in the closet mirror. Not a bad fit. I wasn't completely out of my dream state, otherwise I would have reminded myself how much I hated dresses. Frilly, yellow ones at that.

"Thank you." My voice didn't sound like me...I sounded weak and hollowed out. I guessed that wasn't so surprising. In one minute, the shred of emotions and life I'd had were snipped in half. I had nothing more to live for, really. What I didn't realize was that my life had slowly been deteriorating for six years. It hadn't happened in a minute.

"No problem, sweetie. Are you hungry? Ben and Marc are worried sick about your appetite. They say you're looking too thin. They're right. And you were already too thin to begin with." Surprisingly, I wasn't the least bit hungry. I hadn't eaten in days...so what difference did it make if I didn't eat now?

"Not really," I answered.

"Okay, then. I'll leave you be for a little while. There is a brush on the night stand and a couple of books if you feel up to reading. Marc and Cameron are in Cameron's room if you want to go in to see them." I nodded and Andria worriedly left the room. I felt really bad for Andria; she was probably already apprehensive because of her pregnancy and now I was another burden for her. That's all I ever seemed to be - a burden. I tried hard not to think that, but when you're the reason for your entire city's destruction, I don't think you'd be able to help thinking the same thing.

I did as Andria said and brushed my hair and read for a little while. Then I slowly walked to Cameron's room. I took a deep breath and turned the knob. Then I walked in.

Cameron

Marc was sitting on a bed in the middle of the room, looking excited and extremely happy. I bet that kid Cameron was exactly like him. I sat down on the bed next to him, and it was only then that he realized I had come into the room.

"Creed!" he cried. "Are you okay? How are you feeling?" He looked at me with searching eyes.

"I'm...um...doing better. Good."

"Really. I don't believe one word of that. But we'll discuss this later..." he whispered. In a louder tone, he declared, "Meet Cameron."

Cameron had been sitting at a desk typing away rapidly on his computer. He whirled around. Our eyes met. Cameron was taller than Marc, and thin, with big green-blue eyes and a mop of curly brown hair that fell into them. He smiled at me, and revealed a set of straight pearly white teeth. I stared. He stared back.

"Nice to meet you, Creed. Or...in Italian, Ciao."

"Ciao," I breathed. Cameron held me spellbound.

Marc lowered his eyebrows. "Ummmm...we were just talking about those different cave fungi, Creed. You may not be interested," he interrupted.

"She'll be interested," Cameron said quietly.

"You bet," I said back, and settled in for the long run.

Cameron and Marc talked for hours and hours, discussing everything teenage boys would...on a way higher level. Actually, Cameron was 14, one year older than us. But they didn't seem to mind. They went on and on...talking about the book Marc and I had been reading (I put in a few intelligent words here and there about the passages I read), our travels, the cities we had stopped in so far, and about the airport. On this subject, Cameron knew practically everything. I made sure I listened closely.

"The planes here are very big, and so is the airport. There have been quite a few stowaways on many of the planes, but how they do it, I don't know. My guess would be they stole away in the luggage and then were sent to the baggage areas on the plane."

"That's pretty cool," I commented. I made a mental note of his words.

"Yeah. I know. Hey...you guys still haven't seen Rome, right? I can take you around," He was talking to us, but really looking at me. I had a feeling his words really meant: 'are you alright enough?'

We shook our heads 'yes', so Cameron called to his mom. She came running, thinking maybe something had happened, but when Cameron told her his idea, she thought it was delightful and left us alone to prepare.

Cameron grabbed a leather sack and stuffed it with snacks, a camera, a mini first-aid kit, and a guidebook. He took my hand and led me out of the room and down the hall.

"Where do you want to go?" Cameron asked a very unhappy -looking Marc.

"I don't care. Creed, what about you?"

"Hmmmm..." I thought about it carefully. Finally, I decided. "Let's visit the Colosseum first, and then we can visit the Sistine Chapel. I really want to see those paintings on the ceiling."

"They're very famous. Michelangelo had to lie on his back on some scaffolding in order to paint them. Actually, he really didn't want to paint them. However, the king at the time ordered him to, so he had no choice."

"That's so mean! Yet really interesting. I bet he put a lot of passion into his work."

"You bet!" We started walking, and I thought I heard Marc say something like: 'You're putting a lot of *passion* into this conversation!' But I wasn't sure. Marc tends to mumble when he's mad.

We caught a tour bus and Cameron went to speak to the driver in Italian. When he came back to sit with us, the bus driver turned around and winked at me. Then he cried:

"First stop...the Colosseum!" We cheered. I liked that bus driver. Better yet, it was Cameron who had arranged it.

"What did you say to him?" I whispered.

"Yeah! It looked like you might have hypnotized the poor guy," Marc said sarcastically. I wondered what was going on with him.

"I told him we had two passengers who were new to Rome, and one of them had just been seriously injured in the mountains. I guess he felt bad for you, Creed, so he asked me where you wanted to go and I told him: 'First stop...the Colosseum.'"

"You're a genius!"

"OH...it was nothing."

Marc started mumbling again, but since I couldn't make out anything he was saying, I listened to Cameron more intently. He was telling me some facts about the Colosseum.

"The Colosseum was built by the Flavian emperors - it was a gift to Rome. It took almost 10 years to build! There were three floors and the arches on the first were the main entrances. Games were played and watched at the theater, and 50,000 people could fit into it."

"You're kidding! 50,000?!"

"50,000. I know, right?"

I stared at Cameron incredulously. He knew so much. I felt like I knew so little. Yet, he knew nothing about Pastel, and I knew everything about it. I had a multitude of information and facts inside of me. If only I had the chance to explain it.

"Tell me about Switzerland. That's one place I haven't been, and I'd like to know more about it."

"Well...um...it's sometimes called...the...um...Land of the Switzers! Yes, that's right."

Beside me, Marc laughed.

"She knows nothing about Switzerland. I at least, took the time to learn about our own country." I reddened. Marc was saving me...but it looked like he was trying to embarrass me at the same time. "The languages there are actually similar to your own. German, Italian, and French are the main ones. Switzerland's economy is based on trading and banking internationally. We're known for our exports."

Cameron and I gaped at Marc. How did he know all of that? Surely he couldn't have learned that just from his extra tutoring...?

"But...but...you don't speak Italian!" Cameron sputtered.

"A quanto mi consta, io parlare Italiano," Marc replied effortlessly.

"WHAT? You...you? You speak Italian?" Cameron was amazed.

"Si."

"But I was...I was so sure..." Cameron wrung his hands and looked distraught.

"What?" I asked soothingly. Cameron shook his head as if to bear his thoughts.

"Nothing...nothing. That's so cool, Marc! Do you speak French?"

"Je parler Francais."

"No way!"

Marc and Cameron seemed to have a lot in common, so I left them alone. I sat back against the seat as I listened to them talk what they called 'simple' phrases in Italian and French. It was boring. Plus, I had no idea how Marc had learned those languages. So it was also annoying. Finally, I got an idea. I tugged a handkerchief out of Cameron's bag and pretended to admire it. Then I dropped it. I signaled for the lady in the next seat over to watch it and make sure it was still there.

"OH my! Marc, I lost the handkerchief! I think it fell. *Help me look for it!*" I grabbed Marc by the sleeve and tugged him off the seat. He hit the floor with a thump and we crawled around and looked for the handkerchief. I picked it up and tucked it into my pocket when he wasn't looking. Then I whispered to him,

"You speak other languages??"

He looked at me guiltily.

"Yes. I'll talk to you later...okay?"

"Fine." I pulled out the handkerchief and made sure he knew I'd found it. Then we popped back up and into our seats.

"Found it!" I said cheerfully.

"Meraviglioso," Cameron said in whatever language he was talking. He looked directly at Marc. Marc smiled.

"Excuse me? Excu-so Me-loso...whatever you said," I said politely.

"That sounds nothing like Italian, Creed," Marc said sympathetically. I humphed and sat back in my seat.

"I still don't know what that means," I mumbled.

"*Wonderful.*"

"That's not wonderful! I don't like not knowing things!"

"Creed. The definition of 'meraviglioso' in English is 'wonderful.'"

I humphed again and stared out the window. The sights we passed were blurred because we were going by so fast, but I could still make out the beauty of Rome. The streets were busy and packed, and the buildings and stones were so unique...I came from a place where the only architecture was the kind we had: And that would be a few stone buildings, a couple made of rock and some of clay. Besides those materials, it was hard to get anything else. Actually, I wasn't quite sure myself how those materials had gotten there. I think we may have talked about it in school one day...Christosky Columcloud was in league with a few men down Below who agreed to carry the necessary materials to him in Pastel. They were sworn to secrecy. Actually, Columcloud may have had to kill them when they were finished with the job. Just kidding.

They carried the materials in planes and other machines. Thinking about this did not make me happy; it only proved that it could be done. It proved that flying planes could reach our city. And of course, technology would be much better in this day.

Over the speaker in the front of the bus, the driver announced,

"We are now approaching the Colosseum." I felt better once he said this, for Marc and Cameron finally shut up. Normally, I wouldn't mind if they were chattering; but since they were talking another language and I couldn't understand them, it made things a whole lot harder. Besides, I think maybe they were talking about me for a while, for they kept glancing over in my direction frequently.

The bus stopped about 2 minutes later, and we hurried off. The Colosseum was just ahead. I sucked in my breath at the sight of it. The theater loomed high above me, and its beauty and antiquity amazed me. I loved it immediately.

"Come on! Let's go see it!"

Cameron glanced at his watch.

"We don't have long. I didn't realize the Colosseum was farther from home than the Sistine Chapel."

"That's okay. We can go there tomorrow." He smiled and thanked me, then we rushed on.

The Collosseum was magnificent. The tiers stood high above the ground, and the southern side of the old theater was gone. Cameron explained it was because it was ruined in an earthquake, but the ruins were used to build other buildings, like St. Peter's Basilica. Even Marc, who I knew was trying to impress Cameron with his knowledge, seemed impressed. Cameron was just as excited, even though he said he'd been there a million times.

We walked inside and examined the rows and rows of stone seats. We assembled with the other tourists and were led around by a very nice guide. I asked many questions, and all were answered. Afterward, Cameron took us to get some gelato, the Italian ice-cream. It was much denser and creamier than regular ice-cream. It was delicious! I made up my mind then and there that I loved Rome.

We took the bus back to Cameron's house, and Andria was prepared with a lovely Italian dinner of pasta and meat sauce. There was cheese, bread, and butter to go with it. The sauce was creamy and mild, and the pasta tasty and chewy. Yum!

"Did you all enjoy your visit into Rome?" Andria asked with a smile.

"Yes, we did. Very much so," I replied. Ben looked at me inquisitively. "I'll tell you later," I mouthed.

"Mama! Papa! Marc knows how to speak Italian! And French!" Cameron cried excitedly. At the other end of the table, Ben choked.

"What?!" he sputtered.

"Tell you later." Marc mouthed. Ben glanced back and forth between us. I guessed he was wondering just how much we had to tell him.

"Really? Is that so, Marc?" Griffin frowned. He was probably wondering why Marc hadn't already told him so.

"Ci puoi!"

"Wow! What a surprise!" Everyone began talking at once in Italian. At least that time, I wasn't alone. Ben looked just as confused. I think I even spotted a bit of frustration.

After about 15 minutes of non-stop Italian, I cleared my throat. Everyone looked at me.

"This was a *meraviglioso* dinner," I declared. I remembered that meant 'wonderful'. Everyone laughed.

"Yes. Thank you very much for your hospitality," Ben said. "We should probably leave soon."

"No! Not at all! You should stay with us some more so we can show you Rome in all it's glory. It would be our pleasure. Besides, you are no trouble at all. You are so thankful and pleased with everything we do." I gave Andria a grateful look. I didn't want to leave! "Now I'm sure you're all very tired and would like to get to bed. I don't blame you."

"Well, thank you very much! I think we will go to bed. Marc, Creed, let's go."

On our way out of the dining room, Ben nudged us and said, "My room. Get ready first."

I assumed he meant 'get ready for bed,' but I wasn't sure. He didn't look too happy and I had no idea what he could be planning. Marc and I glanced at each other. The only way to find out was to do what he said.

Back in my room, I pulled down my bed covers and got my pillows ready. I hid my pack in the closet, and pulled on some pajamas. I brushed my teeth and hair and washed my face. I was ready. I hurried into Ben's room and found him sitting on his bed, looking over Marc's book. Marc wasn't there yet. What a relief! I had wanted to get there first.

"Creed. You guys said you'd tell me later. Now is later."

"I know, I know. Believe me...I felt well enough. And Cameron packed a first-aid kit."

"I'm worried about you anyway."

"Depression can do a lot of things to a young girl." I tried to find the wisest words to speak, but Ben saw right through me.

"Creed, your condition now is because of a lot of things: Falling off that mountain, hearing that plane, missing your parents, your life...I understand. Everyone goes through the same kinds of things."

"You don't understand! No one has had to go through the kinds of things I've been through. Ben, I am the *destruction* of my city! If it was you, do you think you'd be skipping around outside enjoying life? I don't think so! I'm tired of everyone trying to make me feel better, because it doesn't work!" I turned my back to him and sighed. I was getting tired of the whole trip. The whole darn idea.

Just then, Marc walked in. He saw us, but made no comment. Marc was smart about those sorts of things.

"Yes, Ben?"

"Now is later," Ben repeated. I couldn't help it...my curiosity got the better of me. I flipped around and tried to give Marc the worst stare ever. I think it worked.

"Umm...well, I don't...you might not...understand..." We looked at Marc like he was crazy. He could explain things perfectly! How could we not understand?

"Just tell us, Marc," Ben said quietly.

"I don't know! I really don't! I...I...last night, Cameron let me get on his computer. After he fell asleep, I looked up an Italian English dictionary so I could learn a couple of words. I don't know what happened then. I just...kind of...got sucked in! Every word I saw got locked into place, and after a couple of words had been memorized, something happened, and..."

"And what?" I asked.

"Well, it was like something had been triggered in my brain. Suddenly, I knew Italian. The whole language...after memorizing only a couple of words."

"That's impossible!" Ben breathed. I looked at Marc. Somehow, I didn't quite think what he was saying was impossible.

"What did you do next, Marc?"

"Well, I looked up a French to English dictionary, and after memorizing another couple of words, I suddenly remembered the whole language."

"What do you mean by *'remembered,'* Marc?" Ben asked skeptically. Marc sneered at him. It was the first time I'd ever seen him do that!

"I don't know! After I memorized those first words, I didn't suddenly 'know' the whole language...that's what I thought at first, but after doing it over and over again with all different languages, I realized that it really felt like I was remembering. I was remembering something that had been stored deep, deep down inside of me...and that night, I pulled it up and out." He stared out into the distance. I wanted desperately to know what he was feeling. It must be really weird.

"Marc? How many languages do you speak now?" I asked quietly. He looked at me out of the corner of his eyes.

"Ummmm...about 13. I speak English, French, and Italian, as you already know, as I do German, Spanish, Chinese, Mandarin, Japanese, Thai, Mexican, Greek, Latin, and Mayan. I'm working on the Incan language."

"That's...Marc...how...?!"

"I don't know, Ben. It really isn't something I can explain."

"Obviously!" Ben looked really frustrated. I looked really frustrated. And Marc looked really frustrated. We were a stressed bunch. "Alright, alright. Let's go to bed. Marc, I'm sorry if I sound...mean, or unkind, but you've got to understand that this is hard for me to comprehend."

"I know." Marc bit his lip, then said goodnight and ran out of the room. I watched him out the door.

"Do you think it's possible?" I asked Ben.

"No idea." He put his head in his hands and rocked back and forth. I was too tired to comfort him, so I tiptoed out and shut the door. I hurried back to my room and fell asleep as soon as I hit the mattress.

The Dream

I snuggled under the covers. The bed was *sooooooo* comfortable. That night, I had a strange dream.

I heard voices...they sounded like they were coming from the hallway.

In the dream, I got up and tiptoed to the door. I put my ear to it and listened. I had no idea who was talking.

"Do you have the journal?"

"Yes. It's right here."

"The pilot wants to see it. He thinks it may say something about the city's location."

"Sure. As long as I get it back."

The voices were so strange...they seemed so far away. I felt like I was floating. I whispered,

"It's my journal! It's my journal! I want it back! It's mine!"

I ran back to bed and tossed and turned. Then Marc walked into the room and began talking in 13 different languages...12 I didn't understand. But I caught the words:

"Father and son...didn't catch their names...should have read the entire article...could've figured it out by now..."

I awoke with a start. I was sweating profusely. The sheets had been kicked to the bottom of the bed. My hair was tangled. My pajamas were twisted.

I got up and yawned. What a dream. In a way, it had scared me. I was surprised I had actually remembered it. When I was done getting ready, I went into the kitchen to find everyone already there.

"You ready to have another day of sightseeing?" Cameron asked with a smile.

"Beaucoup amuse!" Marc blurted out.

We all stared at him and he blushed. Quietly, he corrected himself. "Great fun!"

Quickly, I covered for him.

"So, is everything packed? Are we still planning on going to the Sistine Chapel?"

"Si!" Cameron hopped up and went to get his bag. Marc was stuffing food into his mouth. I had a feeling it was because if his mouth wasn't busy, he'd begin talking rapidly in all of his different languages. In a way, I felt sorry for him.

We were ready to go soon, and we made sure we were right on time for one of the tour buses. Again, Cameron worked his magic, and the bus driver didn't even hesitate to go right where we wanted. While Cameron was spinning his web, I talked to Marc quietly.

"Are you okay?"

"No! What do you think? This is nanika I cannot control!" Realizing what he had just done, he grunted and tried again. "This is *something* I cannot control."

"Do you think you'll learn? Or will you continue blurting out random words in different languages forever?" He glared at me, but I was being serious. I really wanted to know. I needed a heads-up if for the rest of my life I should carry around English to Whatever pocket-sized dictionaries.

"I don't think so. If I watch myself, I think I can tame this." He smiled. He had talked in English only.

"You know, Marc, this isn't an entirely bad thing. It will definitely come in handy."

"I know. But I bet you I'll be considered a freak for the rest of my days."

"Ohhh...come on! It's not that bad!"

"Ontou!" he cried sarcastically. (at least, I think he was being sarcastic...) "Oh...uh, that means 'right.' I was being sarcastic."

I saw Cameron coming down the aisle, but I hurried on anyway. "By the way...what language were you speaking?"

"Japanese," he whispered. I giggled.

"All right! Onwards to the Sistine Chapel!" Cameron plopped down beside me and beamed. I thanked him, and he told us it 'was his pleasure.' Boy, was he proper! I just hoped I sounded polite.

On our way there, while Cameron and Marc conversed in Italian, I stared out the window and wondered about a way to find the kid with the journal. We were already behind...and we needed to catch up. Maybe, maybe the planes still hadn't found Pastel. There was a possibility, after all. I wondered what everyone was doing. I was pulled back down to reality when Cameron cried, "Here we are!"

The bus came to a stop and we all piled out. The Chapel was beautiful! We ran towards it and pushed and shoved our way inside. What we saw next made my heart almost stop. The ceiling was covered with exquisite paintings. I had been trying to imagine the look...but I had never imagined it like that. The angels seemed to really fly, the colors and scenes seemed to pop out at us. Everything felt so real, and the bodies of the men and women and angels were so detailed and neat.

"Hey! Takashi!" Cameron's cry was so sudden it made me jump. Marc was at my side in an instant. "Marc, Creed, this is Takashi, a good friend of the family."

Takashi was Japanese, with dark, squinty eyes and a mop of black hair. He waved to Cameron.

"Yoi tame isaimendan temae!" Takashi approached us and shook Cameron's hand.

"I'm sorry guys; he only speaks Japanese. Do you mind if I have a word with him? It's important."

"No problem," Marc replied quickly. He had an almost creepy gleam in his eye, and the edges of his mouth were turned up in the shape of a smile. He looked at me and winked. I finally realized what he was thinking. He must have been suspicious! Cameron didn't know that Marc spoke Japanese also, so Marc could eavesdrop without causing any suspicion.

"Come on, Marc! Isn't that rude? He probably has to ask him something for his father."

"Creed! How can you say that? It's the first time I'll really be able to use my talents." So now he was calling his ability a 'talent.' Did he really believe that? Whatever.

Cameron and Takashi were already meandering through the crowd, and without even looking in their direction or taking his eyes off the ceiling, Marc followed. He turned his back on them and pretended to admire the pictures.

I waited by a pillar and took in as much as I could. If only the people of Pastel could see such beauty! For all of our lives we had been convinced nothing could be as wonderful as our city. Now I was experiencing so much more...I couldn't believe it. Sure, it was wonderful; fantastic, even, but no matter how many ways you described it, even if you used all of the languages in the world, there were probably many things just as beautiful and wonderful Below. I was witnessing one of them.

I caught Marc's eye for a moment. He was lost in thought. He looked dazed. I wondered desperately what Cameron and Takashi could be saying.

◆ ◆ ◆

The Coronation

Helen became Katheryn's top advisor. She accompanied her everywhere, gave her the best advice, and made sure that the paparazzi and fans didn't get too close. She had become a sort of bodyguard.

Katheryn loved having her around. Without either of their parents, both girls only had each other as family. They made sure the other wasn't in any trouble, and if they did happen to fall into a trap, they offered their hand. They were inseparable. With so many tasks and things at hand, it made things much easier if you could turn around and ask your sister for her opinion. For example, the castle was being redone. The throne room was much too sinister, the way King Doulc liked it, and some of the staircases were eerie and strange. So there were constantly maids buzzing around them, asking them which color was best for the new carpet, or which design made the throne 'pop.' They were asked to pick out new wallpapers, and pick the design and glass of the window being put in on the second floor, etc, etc.

It was a dizzying week. Katheryn was told she had to prepare a speech for the people of Pastel, so that she could present it right after her coronation. That was another thing. (There were so many plans being made that finally Helen bought an organizer to keep track.) Katheryn was being called 24-7 down to meet the seamstresses for a fitting. She was to have a whole new wardrobe...with gowns and cloaks and slippers with rubies...and of course she now needed the coronation robe. Helen was able to help her find a picture of their mother's robe at her coronation, and Katheryn modeled it after that.

The robe was a dark emerald green, with a wide, white and gold sash around the middle. Lace embroidered the top half, and the dress had a long train out back. It was beautiful...and Katheryn looked stunning in it. A hairdresser arrived at the palace a couple days later to experiment with her hair, and she decided to swirl it into a gorgeous bun. A gold ribbon would wind around it.

She really was beautiful. Though at the same time, there was an air around both girls...a sad atmosphere lingering above their heads. They had grieved over their father long enough, but the event was still upsetting; now they had no parents at all, and were heaped with responsibility enough for six parents.

In the end, both girls got through that first week unscathed. Shaken, yes, but unharmed and unscathed. Now it was time for the coronation...to be held at 1:00 pm, just after lunch. It would last a long time; first the coronation ceremony, then the traditional speech made by Queen Katheryn, and then the dinner feast held in her honor. It was to be a busy afternoon. The castle was swarming with servants, maids, advisors, and the seamstresses and hairdressers. Katheryn and Helen could find no privacy.

The girls had an early lunch in their room, and Helen congratulated her sister before she was sent away to get dressed and ready.

The girls embraced. "You're going to make a fabulous queen!" Helen whispered into Katheryn's hair. "Make our parents proud!"

Katheryn wiped a tear away as she stood up and held her chin high. She looked back at her younger sister one last time, time enough to whisper, "I will." Then she hurried out the door.

It had not even been 30 minutes when Stella came running through the door of Helen's room. Stella was Helen's maid. She liked to call Stella 'her Lady in Waiting.' Stella wasn't fit to be a maid. She was much more, but because she was an orphan, too, it was hard for her to find work and a place to stay. The castle offered that much. Stella followed Helen everywhere, at a distance so Helen wouldn't feel as if her privacy was being invaded, or over-crowded.

Stella had dark hair that fell past her shoulders, and her eyes were a shocking green. They sparkled when you looked at them, and they had small flecks of gold around their rims. Her skin was tan, and she had a light laugh. She was a beautiful girl, and sometimes Helen felt self-conscious around her. Stella was loyal, too, and Helen trusted her immensely.

"What is it, Stella?" Today, Stella didn't look as groomed as she usually did. In fact, she looked worried, scared. Her hair fell into her eyes and she was breathing in racked breaths. Helen spotted a small tear in the hem of the girl's dress.

"Oh, Princess Helen! I'm so glad I found you!" Helen stood up and grabbed Stella's arm. She led her to the bed and made sure she had gotten a glass of water before letting her continue.

"Now, tell me. What's wrong?" Helen was worried now, too. What if Stella had bad news about the coronation? Or what if Ryn had collapsed on the stairs? What if she was dying?

"It's nothing to do with Ryn or the coronation, ma'am. It has to do with your father...and his death." Helen froze. She glanced away and in a strained voice asked, "What about him?"

"I wanted to tell you, Helen! I really did! But I was scared and then it was stolen..."

"Tell me *NOW*, Stella."

"As your father was being cornered by the man with the dart, he had time to pick up a piece of paper and write you a message. I found it, and before I had a chance to show you in private, it was stolen by someone else."

"What did it say?" Now Helen was the one fighting for breath. In the wrong hands, the message could prove deadly.

"It said: 'Find the Keeper.'"

An hour later, the throne room was filled with people. Important people. Helen and the advisors in front, the scientists and lords and rich guys farther back. The music began to play. The minister stood at the front next to the throne, the throne with the crown sitting on its seat. He held the Bible in his hand, and a piece of paper.

As the music got louder, the guests turned in their seats to look at the double doors through which Katheryn was supposed to enter.

At the climax in the music, the doors swung open and in strode Queen Katheryn, her hair pulled back into a bun, her eyes sparkling, the emerald train of her dress swishing over the floor behind her. She walked slowly to the throne, past the rows and rows of seats, past the columns of the hall, past the flowers set in the aisle, to the minister who couldn't seem to take his eyes off of her. When she reached him, she turned and faced the audience.

"Katheryn, my dear, do you accept this responsibility as Queen?"

"Of course I do. I am ready, minister."

"Then you shall prosper forevermore and your soul will linger with the hearts of your people. Sit." He picked up the crown in his hands.

Katheryn, very gracefully, sat down in the throne, her back erect and her dress flowing onto the floor.

"You are now...officially...Queen of Pastel! All hail Queen Katheryn!" Slowly, the minister placed the bejeweled crown upon Katheryn's head. She smiled, and Helen thought she saw a tear linger on Katheryn's face before she wiped it away.

Once the crown had been placed, cries of "All hail Queen Katheryn!" filled the room. Helen was the loudest. Katheryn smiled - a real smile - and silenced the people in the hall.

"Thank you. Now if you could exit to the right, there has been a section roped off for you all outside to listen to my acceptance speech." Slowly, the crowd exited single file, row by row, and Helen raced up to her sister. They hugged each other tightly. When they released themselves, Helen saw tears in her sister's eyes. Hopefully, and most likely, they were tears of joy. Helen was going to tell her about their father's message, but didn't want to ruin the moment. Plus, she didn't want to have to explain anything. The girls exited out the back door and took a short cut to the balcony, where two servants and bodyguards were waiting. One held a microphone, and he handed it to Katheryn when she arrived.

Applause broke out when Katheryn stepped onto the balcony. Practically everyone in Pastel was present, and

Helen thought she saw Mr. and Mrs. Skye applauding, too, just below, but she wasn't sure. Katheryn silenced the crowd once more and began her speech.

"People of Pastel. I thank you for supporting me as Queen, and I hope that I do not disappoint you. What happened to my father was a very sad tragedy, and hopefully won't happen to me if I am able to communicate with you more and really listen to you. Hopefully, by the end of my reign, I will be able to call you *My People*." The speech was not a long one, but a very precise one, and Katheryn knew what she wanted. Another round of applause filled the air. It sounded like a clap of thunder, and if it was indeed loud enough for the people Below to hear, that was probably what they thought it really was.

◆ ◆ ◆

Long Lost

Marc sidled away from Creed, farther and farther into the crowd, closer and closer towards Cameron and the suspicious Takashi dude. Marc didn't trust them. How 'important' could a pleasant conversation be? But maybe it wasn't supposed to be pleasant.

Ever since Marc had found his new talent, he had felt lost and confused. It was so embarrassing to blurt out parts of conversations and sentences in different languages. Especially if it was Mayan. But now he had a chance to prove that he could really use the 'talent' and it wasn't just something that would make him feel awkward for the rest of his life.

Marc backed so close to the two that he almost knocked Takashi over. There he held his ground, put his hands in his pockets, and admired the ceiling between two fat ladies.

Takashi: "I talked to your father yesterday."

Cameron: "I heard," he sounded annoyed. Marc wondered why. He inched closer.

Takashi: "You did? So you know what he wants?"

Cameron: "Of course I know what he wants! He wants...he wants to publish the journal. He wants to send up another plane. He wants to get paid for the find and he wants to investigate the city...if he finds it." Marc gasped. Could they be talking about Creed's journal?

Takashi: "Cameron, you know what's best. What do you want?"

Cameron was silent for a moment. He stared at the ceiling. No one would ever guess he was really just thinking. "I want...I didn't want such publicity. But I guess that's stupid. Do you think that's stupid? I mean...what if there is a city up there...do they want us scouting around in their privacy?"

Takashi: "This is a major find, Cameron. Publicity is something almost everyone wants. Sometimes, I can't figure you out. But I guess you've decided, haven't you?"

Cameron: "I can't turn on my father. He's giving the journal to the pilot, and after I get it back, we're sending it to a publisher."

Takashi: "Come on, Cameron. Don't be selfish."
Cameron gave a small laugh. Marc had a feeling Cameron didn't really mean it.

Cameron: "I know. It was nice seeing you, too, Takashi. I'll see you around."

Takashi vanished into the crowd and Cameron ran smack into Marc. Marc had to think of something...he had to get the information he had just learned to Creed. She would be amazed...she might not even believe it. But to Marc, it made perfect sense. A father and son...the newspaper article they had found mentioned so. Griffin was an archaeologist. Cameron wanted to be an archaeologist. What else would interest them more than a journal describing an unknown civilization?...in the sky?

"Uhhhhh....Cameron! I have to go to the bathroom. Is there one around?"

"Yeah, sure. Follow me." Cameron and Marc wove their way through the crowd. Marc waved to Creed and motioned for her to stay where she was. Finally, they reached a bathroom. Marc noted the light switch as they walked in. Cameron decided he would go, too, and they both entered a stall. Once Marc heard Cameron pull his pants down, he burst out of his stall, flicked off the light switch, and hurried out. It would take Cameron a while to figure out what happened, but not long. Marc barely had enough time.

He ran through the crowd and over to a stunned Creed.

"Where's Cameron?" she asked immediately.

"No time!" Marc panted. He doubled over and tried to breathe. It was already enough that Creed really seemed to like Cameron. Wait until she heard. Then he would be the hero and sweep her off her feet...that was enough. Out with the information.

"Marc! What did you do to Cameron?" She took a step back and glared at Marc. He rolled his eyes. It might take a while. Creed was a hard one to convince.

"Cameron has the journal," Marc whispered quietly. He couldn't beat around the bush. Cameron would have found his way out by then. He was probably running towards him at this very moment.

"What?" Creed stared at him and shook her head. Marc fought back a smile. She looked so funny when she did that. She looked so stubborn...so fierce. Normally, he would have backed away before she pounced. But now, he knew she wasn't going to pounce on *him*.

"Cameron and Griffin are the father and son with the journal. Their names were probably in the paper and we just didn't read enough to see them. Heck...they probably had a picture, too! Anyways, they're planning to send up another plane soon. Griffin's going in the plane, and taking the journal with him. Then they're going to try to publish it."

"PUBLISH IT! PUBLISH *MY* JOURNAL!" Creed was almost screaming. Bystanders had turned to look and were now staring at them. Marc gave a nervous laugh and pushed her behind a statue.

"*Your* journal?" a cold voice asked. Marc whipped around and followed Creed's gaze. Cameron.

For a whole minute, a minute that seemed like an eternity, the three just looked at each other. Each had something different on their face. Creed wore an angry expression; yet guilty; yet anxious. Cameron wore something similar. His eyebrows were down, and his brown hair fell into his face. He was frowning and looked extremely sinister. Marc crossed his arms and tried to burn a hole in Cameron's face with his malice. It didn't work. Finally, Creed spoke up.

"Yes. My journal," she said defiantly. Cameron broke out into a grin.

"You're...you're serious?" Cameron looked at Creed skeptically. She nodded. Marc frowned suspiciously. Something was up. Why was Cameron acting so weird? Surely Creed had put her name in the journal?

"Cameron...you're not telling us something," Marc spoke up. Cameron looked at him accusingly. He laughed sarcastically and sucked in his breath. Then he shook his head and laughed again.

"*I'm* not telling *you* something? Don't you think it's the other way around? Are...are you from...?"

Creed bit her lip and looked at Marc. He stared back and they tried to communicate wordlessly. Cameron was getting impatient. Finally, Creed just sighed and broke down. Marc nodded and gave her a look that said: It's okay.

"Cameron...there's something we need to tell you." They pulled Cameron out of the Chapel and down the steps.

They found a quiet street and sat down by a garbage can. Cameron looked at them strangely.

Once they had gotten comfortable, they told Cameron everything. Starting at the very beginning. Creed and Marc poured out the story, not missing a detail. They told of Creed's life of denial, of Marc's being an orphan, of how they found Ben and how Creed escaped her guards and journeyed to the World Below. They told of how they had traveled, describing their time with Griffin, Cameron's father, and how Creed had fallen and of everything after that.

"Can you puto it?" Marc groaned and covered his face with his hands. "Sorry!" he whispered. "Latin."

Cameron, who hadn't said anything yet, just looked at Marc with amazement.

"You're a Communicator, aren't you?" he asked in awe. Marc lifted his head and raised an eyebrow.

"A what?" he asked.

"A Communicator. I read about them in the journal."

Creed frowned. "I didn't write anything about a Communicator in my journal! I don't even know who they are!" Marc and Creed watched a smile play on Cameron's lips.

"Right," he said quietly. "Because it's not your journal."

♦ ♦ ♦

Cecilia

I stared at Cameron. None of us spoke. Not my journal? Why wasn't it my journal? And...most importantly...if it wasn't my journal, who's was it and where was mine?

"It...it has to be my journal!" I stuttered. I couldn't believe what was happening. Why was it happening? We had finally found a lead, and then we discovered that it was a false one.

"I'm sorry, Creed, but it's not your journal. It's Cecily's."

"Who's?"

"Cecily's. By the way...what is your city called?"

"Pastel," Marc and I answered together.

"Oooohhhh...wow! This is sooooo cool! What a find." Cameron smiled triumphantly, as if he had just won the lottery.

"Where does Cecily live? I don't know of her," I asked. It was all very confusing. Marc was staring at the ground. He was entwining his fingers so furiously I thought they might fall off. What was he doing? I had a feeling he was on to something.

"Creed...if the journal fell from the sky, and we don't know a Cecily...then...then there must be...another city in the sky!" Marc and I fell silent. It was impossible. Utterly and totally impossible. I think I almost fainted, but Marc caught me in his arms. Cameron peered at us anxiously.

"You guys don't know of Scharr?" he asked incredulously. "Wow! I thought you guys would know for sure!"

"Scharr?" I repeated. I didn't like the sound of that city.

"Yeah. Cecily lives there. By the sound of it, I don't think she likes it much. However...I think she knows about Pastel. She and her...father. Which probably means that the rest of the city, does, too."

"Really?" I asked. The only thing I liked about that new development was the fact that my city wasn't in danger after all. Then that hope had been shattered, too. When Cameron saw my expression, he added hastily,

"It doesn't mention Pastel directly. I...I don't know how to describe it. Thankfully, my father overlooked that detail."

"So you're going to help us? You won't tell your dad?" Marc cried hopefully. We bit our lips and waited with bated breath. He turned pale, and glanced away.

"I...I'll help you." For a minute, Cameron looked embarrassed. Then, he hopped up. "My father can't know. Pretend you're still kids from Switzerland, sister and brother and the children of Ben. Alright?"

"Fine," I agreed with a sigh of relief. I felt so much better.

"But...but we still have to stop that plane! What if your father finds the wrong city? Or both? Even if it's not my journal, I know just how that girl must be feeling. We can't let either city be found."

Cameron and Marc nodded their approval. Silently, we trotted out from behind the trash can and went to find a tour bus. A million thoughts were whirring around inside my head. When I looked at Marc, he seemed lost in thought too. I couldn't believe it. So my journal hadn't been found. My city wasn't in danger. There was another city in the sky, Scharr. And the girl Cecily lost her journal just like me and now it was in the hands of none other than Cameron, son of Griffin who was planning to find the city and scout around there. We weren't going to let that happen. I didn't know how, but I vowed to myself then and there that I would keep the archaeologist out of that city.

The tour bus was comfortable and eased my tense muscles. Those minutes in the Sistine Chapel had left me dazed and a bit scared. Once everything had been sorted out, I felt a whole lot better. Apparently, Marc didn't feel as good as I did. His brow was still furrowed and he was staring out the window, oblivious to mine and Cameron's conversation.

"Marc? Are you okay?" I asked.

"Yeah...yeah, I'm fine." He continued staring out the window until he asked, "Cameron? What's a Communicator? You didn't quite explain that to me."

Cameron laughed, then patted Marc on the back.

"Don't worry! It's something to be proud of. Communicators are very rare. I'm not sure I know how to explain it...in a way that makes sense to you. You'll have to read Cecily's journal. It's really interesting. You see, the whole reason I really went along with dad's whole crazy plan was because I hoped to one day meet Cecily. I mean, you've got to admit, we're kind of connected now."

I frowned. Why wasn't I the one who was 'connected' to Cameron? That Cecily was really lucky.

"You'll let us read the journal?" Marc asked excitedly. Cameron nodded.

"My dad had it for a while, to show the pilot of the plane he's going to be using. But he gave it back to me for a while because he doesn't need it. And then I'll have to give it back to him when the plane takes off." I couldn't help but feel excited, too. It wasn't every day you got to read someone else's personal thoughts. Especially if they lived in another city in the sky!

We were home in time for lunch, and Andria had some homemade pizza ready. It was really good, but Marc and I were anxious to see the journal. Finally, lunch was over, and with the grown ups watching us suspiciously, we hurried into Cameron's room. He grabbed his chair and stood on it. He pulled down a couple of books from his book shelf, then revealed a tiny cabinet behind them.

"I built it myself." He said with a hint of pride in his voice. "This is where I keep all of my secret stuff. I had to carve a hole in the wall, which was harder than you'd imagine, and then I had to make a door for it. Ahhh...here it is. Writings of Cecilia."

He pulled down a really pretty leather book and placed it on the bed. It looked nothing like mine, nothing at all. The soft leather was a dullish red, with a brown leather strap tied around it. He untied the strap and carefully opened it up. The pages were turning yellow, but they were still crisp and in perfect shape. The letters covering the page were neat, and in a strange way, really pretty. They were dainty and perfect. I wondered if this Cecilia was a sappy girly girl. I hoped not. I didn't take a fancy to those kinds of girls.

"Read the first page, and then I'll show you the passage about Communicators."

He flipped to the first page, and handed the book to us. Without hesitation, we began to read.

Journal of Cecilia (Cecily, please)

First writing...
Cecilia is my birth name, but I don't think it sounds like me at all, so I have people call me Cecily. 'Cecily' has a nice ring to it. Not one of those names that defines you right away, if you know what I mean. For example - 'Ashley' is one of those names that says right off that you're a girly girl. A prissy girl. Someone who likes frills and nail-polish. That, or your mom is the prissy one.

I live in Scharr. Notice I don't say 'I was born here' or 'Scharr is my birth place.' It may sound really strange, but it's true...I was abducted at birth. From where, I don't know. Elias isn't stupid. He even told me so; his exact words: "Cecily, I would never have kidnapped you from the place in which we live. It would be too easy to trace me. You've learned for yourself...telling the police you were kidnapped at birth is no good because they know I've had a child. They don't know that the child wasn't you." I've asked a million times who the child is, but he won't tell me. Probably for good reason, too. The only thing I wonder is this: Why me? Why not his own child?

Elias is my kidnapper. He is a doctor. I call him 'O Evil One' behind his back. Actually, though, he's a good doctor. That's why no one suspects him. He lives on the outskirts of Scharr, and although he's really rich and practically famous, he and his wife Clara live in a moderately sized home. They've had two daughters since they kidnapped me. Eva and Faye. I don't think Eva's real name is Eva - I'm pretty sure its 'Evil'. It's a perfectly honest mistake. She's a sweet child at first sight. She demands attention and is a real show-stopper. She's brilliant in every way. But really and truly, she's cruel and twisted. (I think she might have gotten that trait from Elias.) It's strange, because I'm pretty sure she loves me. She has long, dirty-blond hair and magnificent green eyes. Freckles cover her cheeks, just like her mom, and when she smiles, its either to put on a show or because she just thought of something terrifically terrible. She's 10 now, and Faye is 8. Faye scares me. She's practically a ghost. I'll be writing in my journal and she's suddenly just there. Standing behind me, looking at me with the most innocent - and creepy - expression you've ever seen. She's quiet as a mouse, and perfect for sending on spying sessions. She looks just like Eva except for a couple of minor differences. They look so alike sometimes I think they might be twins. Faye's hair is straighter. Pin straight. I've tried to put barrettes in it before, but they slide out. It's smooth and shiny. She doesn't have freckles, like Eva. And her eyes are hazel. Both girls are amazingly thin. Sometimes I wish I looked like them.

I don't have any friends. The kids here think I'm too strange. It's probably because I tell them my story, hoping one of them will believe me, but it's hopeless. I'll be stuck here forever. The only proof I have is this: The words Elias tells me. I know they're true...he loves to torture me...but they make sense, too. I look nothing like him and Clara. Nothing. Clara's got beautiful hazel eyes (Faye got those) and dark brown hair that falls down her back. (It's strange that neither Eva nor Faye have their parent's hair color.) Her few freckles make her look young. Elias is handsome, but in my eyes, he's a monster. Elias has green eyes that sparkle in the sun, like me, and that's why some think we look alike, but that's it. Otherwise, we're opposites. He has coal black hair like a raven that he slicks back, even though it looks better when it's curly. His skin is pale, and he has no freckles at all like Clara. His smile is kind of freaky...one of those dead-on evil smiles. You'd know it if you saw it.

I'm a different story. I have wavy, sandy blond hair that falls to my shoulders, crystal green eyes with a rim of gold around the edges, and dimples. I hate those.

End of First writing

I laughed when I finished reading. Marc and Cameron just smiled.

"Do you really believe that, Cameron?" I asked through my giggles. He nodded. I shut up.

"She's got perfect evidence. You have to read on. There are a lot of things that get explained. Turn to page...7 or 8...and read the Third Writing. It's good. You know, Creed, she sounds a lot like you."

"Do you want to read one of Creed's journal pages?" Marc asked, trying to suppress his laughter. "She wrote it when she was seven!"

"Ummm...not today! We'll save that for sometime else, okay, Cameron? Alright, let's read." I blushed a deep red. I was not going to let Cameron read my journal. No way.

Third writing

So far, I've mostly written about my life. Now I need to write more about my city, Scharr. As much as Scharr may be evil, it's still my city and I've grown very fond of it.

Scharr is sinister. The buildings there are so tall you can't see their tops. The security system is unbeatable, and don't even get me started on the jail. It's the worst place to be in all of Scharr. Anyway, the city is a hard place to escape. I've tried, believe me. I've tried climbing the wall, getting past the security to find the keys to the gate...it's all no use. The only way I'm ever leaving Scharr is if someone rescues me from the outside. Or if someone finally believes me and arrests Elias. He deserves to be locked in jail for the rest of his wretched life. Yes...that's it. One day I will make sure he is arrested. That is my new goal.

There are several types of people in Scharr...most are usually serious and sarcastic. I have to admit I can be that way sometimes. Alright...a lot of the time. But there are special people, too. Take

Communicators, for instance. They can speak every language in the world. Even Below languages, like Italian or French or Dutch. Communicators may not know who they are for some time. The average age range is usually 11-14. They might hear snippets of another language and realize they actually understand it. That's the common way they find out about their abilities. Then, through practice, they can uncover and unharness their talents. At first, they may have to look up certain words of a language to 'remember' it. Once they've gotten their power under control, however, they can reach inside themselves to speak the language and 'learn' it. It's kind of a complicated thing to explain. Only Communicators themselves know what's it like to understand any language in the world without having to learn it. I know so much about them because I've always longed to be one. They're so cool...and they're perfect for eavesdropping and spying.

Cameron glanced at Marc at that point.

There are other sorts of talents in Scharr, too. There are those who are Analytical, and the Puzzlers. Those who are Analytical can analyze anyone's feelings. In the blink of an eye they can know what causes the feelings. They can read anyone's expressions thoroughly, and you can't escape their impenetrable gaze. They're quite annoying people. Fortunately, they're shy and quiet and don't like to be disturbed much. Then there are the Puzzlers. It's kind of a funny name - actually, I think all of the names are quite stupid - but the Puzzlers themselves are not. They're people you don't want to mess with. It's strange, because their talent has nothing to do with feelings and people. At least not much, anyway. They can solve any riddle you give them in the blink of an eye. An extremely hard riddle for regular people is an easy warm-up problem for a Puzzler. You may not think this gift would come in handy, but actually, mankind speaks mostly in riddles. When you're describing something to someone - you're giving them a mystery, clues for them to imagine and piece together. Puzzlers can figure out the true meaning behind anyone's words. They can read expressions and understand someone's true feelings. Puzzlers are rare in Scharr. I wish I was one. I have no extraordinary talent. Elias argues with me about that - he says I can win any argument with my arrogance and cleverness.

End of Third writing

"So? What do you think?" Cameron was speaking to both of us, but I was the only one listening. Marc was rereading the passage about the Communicators.

"I'm a Communicator. A Verbindung. (German)," Marc whispered. "Jeg blikk tale."

"Huh?" Cameron and I asked.

"'I can speak', I said. In Norwegian. I learned it last night." Marc looked happy with himself. So proud and confident...I hadn't felt that way in a really long time.

We talked a little longer, read a little longer, but we couldn't find anything else of importance. Besides, Cameron would've already found something.

We told Ben after dinner that night, and he was amazed. At first, he cried,

"That's it! Cameron! I should've known. Yes, he's the one alright."

"No, actually. Cameron doesn't have my journal," we explained. "I wonder why you thought Cameron had read my journal."

"Well...I know now that Cameron definitely fits the person I was thinking of. So, if I was wrong, then no one must have read your journal, Creed!"

He congratulated Marc, but seemed worried about the fact that there was another city in the sky. An 'evil' one at that.

The only thing we kept secret was the part about stopping the plane. We had no idea how to do it, and Ben would only stop us. It seemed the right thing to do.

After we'd gone to bed, we snuck into Cameron's room to talk to him. He told us he had already conversed with his father, and he was planning to send up the search plane the next afternoon. If we had any chance of stopping them, we'd have to do it the next morning. Cameron decided we'd station ourselves in different spots in the airport. Two of us would bribe someone to show us the plane, and then the other would follow close behind. While the person from the airport wasn't looking, the other kid would slit the airplane tires. I didn't quite understand what else they would do, but Marc did. Apparently he had read up on planes when the news came on that night. That night when our whole adventure had started. He tried to explain it to me afterwards, but I finally convinced him it was no use. All I needed to understand was that they'd be doing something to the engines.

The next morning, we gathered around the breakfast table. Andria couldn't make it because she was too tired. Griffin said she was resting and would probably be going to the hospital someday soon. Cameron looked worried, but Griffin didn't seem to be. He looked as if he had a lot on his mind.

"Cameron...I have to go to the airport sometime today to talk to the pilot of the plane we're sending up, alright? I don't want you kids going too far away from the house."

Cameron straightened and almost choked on his food if it wasn't for Marc, who had to clap him on the back. Obviously, our plan of going to the airport might take longer than just the morning. We couldn't take any risks if Griffin was involved. Hopefully, though, he would be in a totally different part of the airport.

"Oh...yeah, sure, dad." Cameron glanced at us. We tried to give each other messages through our eyes, but Griffin and Ben were still looking at us. So we waited until breakfast was over.

Once again, we piled in on Cameron's bed. His hair was falling into his face, but he pushed it away before speaking. He said we didn't have time to worry about his father. We had to go along with the plan anyway. I could tell Marc was thinking the same thing, but for once, I wasn't. It was going to take a lot of nerve...and if there was the possibility that Griffin would interfere, I didn't want to take the chance.

Cameron pulled on his sweatshirt sleeve. He looked down at it, lost in thought. In the end, we decided (even me) to go through with it without hesitation. Sure, we had to be careful, but they were right. Besides - Griffin was going sometime that afternoon. Hopefully, we would be done with our job and on our way back.

The bus ride down to the airport wasn't too bad. I thought about our task all the way there. Marc and I had never been to an airport before, so it would be a new experience. Something to put in my journal when I got back. (I had a lot to put in my journal).

The air outside had suddenly gotten colder, and so I was wearing a warm jacket, thanks to Andria. We thought it was going to be really sunny, but apparently we were wrong. So we left with warm jackets and sunglasses. A strange mix. It was so foggy outside that I didn't even see the airport approaching until it was right in front of us. I had imagined it much differently. It was so big...I had imagined it much smaller. From the building extended long driveways that forked out amidst plains and plains of grass. Some of the planes stood on these driveways, looking tall and proud and ready to take flight.

"Those 'driveways' are called 'runways,'" Cameron told us. "We're looking for one with a much smaller plane. The one we're looking for usually carries around...I don't know...two to four passengers."

I nodded and continued concentrating on the runways. They were so big. Just then, I saw one of the planes slowly begin to roll down the runway. It picked up speed, faster and faster, until, just like the saying, it was flying. It had just lifted off the ground and sped into the sky. Ascending higher and higher, just like the one I had seen on our way there. It was an ugly sight to me...yet magnificent and graceful in it's own way.

"Come on, Creed." Cameron took my hand and pulled me off the bus. I had to admit, I felt better when he did that. The airport had seemed like some monster before, and then it was a little less scary.

Once we reached the lobby, Cameron and I hurried up to the desk through the swarms of people.

"Excuse me...but this young girl here..." Cameron pointed at me, and I waved. "...is very interested in the plane going up to search for that civilization."

The woman smiled. Obviously the airlines were getting a lot of publicity with the whole thing Griffin was planning.

"Would you like me to show you around?" She asked sweetly. The woman had a short blond bob and blue eyes. Her smile was perfect, and she looked picture-perfect, too. Her dimples showed when she smiled, and her eyes sparkled. Her lips were plump and rosy pink. She wore a diamond clip in her hair and when she pushed it behind her ear, I caught a glimpse of bright pink fingernails.

"Could you? Oh, that would be wonderful!" I cried. That had been easy. Too easy. Cameron winked at me, and I in turn winked at Marc, who was 'observing' the airplanes outside.

We followed behind the woman as she clicked down the hallway, precarious in her 3-inch high heels. Her uniform was sassy and sweet, so I suspected she had 'renovated' it. The button down white shirt now had pink initials on the pocket, and around the collar was a pearl necklace. The pants were cropped with pink stitching down the sides; barely visible. Her shoes had tiny pink rhinestones in the straps. She must have really liked pink.

Inconspicuously, Marc followed us through the airport. There were many different rooms and hallways and stairs leading to other floors and waiting areas and ticket centers. I saw many a snack booth, with ice-cream or hot-dogs or hamburgers or french fries.

The woman was a fast talker. She spoke on and on about the plane while I tried to listen.

"Thisplaneissomethingthatwe'vebeenworkingonforawhil esothatitwillflyhigherthanmost. Ithinkitwillbeverysuccessfulandthemanthatownsit-   Griffin-isveryproudofitalso. Hissonistheonewhofoundthiswonderfuljournal,soI'mhappyf orhim,too!"

Soon, we reached an empty waiting room leading out to a small plane. it was refreshing, after looking at so many gigantic ones. She led us through a small tunnel out onto the runway. The plane stood before us, and if it had looked small before... it looked a lot bigger. I knew it was just from standing closer up, but it was still a bit intimidating.

Cameron and I then began asking our questions. We asked as many as we could, taking turns and pointing in opposite directions so that she couldn't see Marc tampering away on the other side.

"So...exactly how high is this plane planning to go?"

"In what direction is it headed?"

"Who is the pilot? Is he well known? What school did he attend?"

"How do I become a pilot? Where would I find more information on jets like these?"

We kept the woman, Julia, talking for a long time before she finally stopped to take a breath. I heard a slight sound, and kicked up another stream of questions before she could do anything about it. We were almost done - with a clean getaway in sight - when suddenly, one of Julia's answers stopped us short. Cameron had just asked her about those who were planning to go up in the plane.

"Well, I'm pretty sure Mr. Griffin himself is going up in the plane. He's been a little disappointed in the other planes' success so far..." At that she frowned before going on, "So this time he wants to go up, too. Ahhhh...here he comes now." She smiled fondly at the man and waved. "MR. GRIFFIN!" she cried. She jumped up and down until her hair fell into her face.

Cameron gasped. He turned to me and gestured for me to follow him. He hurried behind Julia and took off his jacket.

"Pull your hair up into your hood!" he hissed. As quickly as I could, I tied my hair into a bun and pulled my hood well over my face. Cameron stuck a pair of sunglasses at me, and I shoved them onto my face. Cameron, who had been wearing a sweater, tore it off and stuffed it down his shirt. By bunching it up appropriately, it made him look chunkier. He pulled his socks up and matted down his hair, with my help.

Hopefully, our disguise would be enough to fool Griffin for the time being.

"Julia! So nice to see you!" Griffin ran his fingers through his dark hair and smiled. As he approached, he looked the jet plane up and down, scrutinizing it thoroughly. Julia waited with bated breath. I wondered if maybe Griffin hadn't seen the plane yet.

"It looks good," he finally declared. "I think it should work." Only then did he seem to notice us. Cameron tried to hide behind me, so that Griffin wouldn't see us too clearly, but Griffin looked past me anyway. "Who are they?" he asked.

"Oh...just innocent kids who wanted to see the plane. I've been telling them all about it for at least...oh my gosh! It's been an hour! An HOUR! I need to get back to my shift! Oh my gosh! Griffin, I mean...Mr. Griffin, sir, could you please escort these kids to the parking lot? I think another bus will be here shortly." Without awaiting a reply, Julia ran away, her short bob flying in the wind. At one point I think she almost tripped; it wouldn't have been a surprise, what with those high heels; but I wasn't sure. I was too far away.

Griffin turned to us. He looked at us strangely, in two different ways: One, as if we were ridiculously dressed children (which we probably were), and Two: almost as if he had seen is before; perhaps in some strange dream, maybe. Cameron shuffled his feet. I whistled. I was a really good whistler.

We stood there like that for almost two minutes long before Griffin said,

"Do I know you?"

"I...I don't think so. I mean - I don't know you. Sir," I said in the gruffest voice I could muster. Cameron said nothing. "He's mute," I said, and pointed over my shoulder.

My head was racing. How would we get rid of Griffin? How could we get him to go away? Just then, Griffin whipped around. I had heard it too. We all had. The clank of metal against metal. Griffin glanced at us, then rounded the plane.

♦ ♦ ♦

Marc had done just what he'd needed to do. He'd followed behind the girly tour guide and Creed and Cameron, he'd snuck to the other side of the plane, and he'd begun tampering at once. First he slit the tires. Cameron had lent him his pocket knife, and with one flick of his wrist, the thing was shining in the light overhead. Marc was glad it was so foggy...otherwise, the guide and the others probably would've been able to see his shadow.

He wasn't sure whether he should do the tires closest to Creed and Cameron. At first, he'd decided not to. Then he'd crawled underneath and slit the tires from a distance. There was a pretty big space underneath the plane, one glance down and the guide probably would have spotted him. But he was careful to stay quiet...oh so quiet.

The lady had talked on and on and on as he made sure to do some damage. He was pretty sure it was illegal to do something like that...but you had to do what you had to do. He found several compartments that he made a mess of, and after a while made sure the last of the air was out of the slit tires. He was pretty proud of his work. He was about to give his signal - a soft bird cry - when he heard the girl say: "Ahhhh...here he comes now." She was talking about Griffin, of course. He'd heard that, too. What were they to do then? He was sure Cameron and Creed would make disguises, then fool Griffin. But how would he get past Griffin? He had nothing to work with.

He heard the woman run off, and he heard the silence that followed. He heard Creed explain that Cameron was mute...she was hilarious...when the plan came to him. There was nothing else he could do. He closed his eyes and took a deep breath, then left some of Cameron's tools behind. He scurried under the plane, and then clanked two of them together as loudly as he could. As soon as Griffin began walking, and rounded the nose, Marc shot out from underneath, pulled his hood up so Griffin couldn't see his face, and ran. The others caught on quickly. They ran as fast as they could, and he could tell they were gaining headway. The plane was farther away from the tunnel than they had remembered, but at least it was there all the same.

They hurried inside the tunnel and practically fell into the airport waiting room. There they crouched. They peeked out the window. They saw Griffin - holding the tools in his hands - stomping around and looking extremely mad. But they weren't safe yet. Griffin picked up a walkie-talkie attached to his belt and spoke into it rapidly. They didn't even stay around to learn what he had said. They pulled off their disguises and made new ones by switching hats, glasses, and jackets. It worked, for they snuck past Julia. She was scanning the entire waiting room, searching for two kids. (She didn't yet know about Marc.)

They had almost left the waiting room when Griffin busted out through the tunnel. He didn't have time to see them for they had already gone. The next waiting room looked just like the first. The only difference was that it had an escalator to the second floor. They clambered up and found somewhere to hide, where, luckily, no employees were around. Only the plane passengers with their tickets were milling about. They lingered in the crowd and watched several security guards pass by, but that was it. They were safe. Almost. Then they had to get out.

Cameron beckoned for them to follow him into a small coffee shop.

"We'll think of something," he whispered. They sat and thought about their choices.

"Let's find one of those signs with the map on it... and we can plan the most inconspicuous route," Marc suggested. The rest nodded, and gained their breath back from running before they got up. Just then, as they stood up to leave, someone grabbed Creed's arm from behind.

♦ ♦ ♦

Riddle Master

Griffin felt like screaming. He felt like yelling aloud...screaming...stomping...breaking something and throwing a fit. How could that happen? How? And why to him? He had worked so hard to get the plane ready...had been so ready for fame...and now the plane was ruined. Ruined. It would take weeks to repair it, unless he could find another one, which was next to impossible. Whoever had done the job had to have been really smart. Luckily, he had a plan B, but it was not a necessarily good one and he hadn't been set on really using it.

Griffin sighed and stared after the kids running from him. He hated to admit it, but the kids were probably friends of Cameron. Cameron hadn't been too keen on the whole idea of actually sending up a plane. At first, he was really excited, but as he continued to read the journal, Griffin expected he started to really connect with that Cecily girl. Cameron had probably wondered what she would feel like...and because he was so kind-hearted, too kind-hearted, he wanted to protect her. However, he'd never admit that to anyone - Cameron got so touchy and embarrassed when it came to Cecily. And now Creed was in the picture...what had he told her and Marc about the girl?

The plane had definitely been tampered with. The tires had been slit...the engine messed with...the gas drained. He groaned again when he realized how easy it had been for the kid to mess with the plane. How easy it had been for the kids to get away. Julia...he'd have to get her fired. She was too worried about her appearance and impressing everyone. Griffin had learned not to worry...or judge...appearances. Even the most normal looking people might have had a strange past or a secret.

That Ben from Switzerland...and his kids...were people like that.

Griffin squeezed his eyes shut and tried to regain his composure, then fumbled around with his walkie talkie and pressed a number.

"Hello?" came a voice and a wave of static.

"Tino? Is that you?" Griffin asked uncertainly.

"You bet. What's up?" Griffin sighed with relief. If anyone could help him, it was Tino.

"I've got a problem. Three teens just tried to mess with my plane. Julia said one was a girl and one was a boy, but when I got there, I saw two boys and another one messing with the plane. If you see three kids, catch them."

"...hmmm..."

"I assume you'll want to have some fun with them first?"

"Exactly. Over and out."

"Over and out." Griffin switched off the walkie talkie and stuck it back into his pocket. Then he stared up at the sky overhead and yearned to be airborne.

◆ ◆ ◆

Cameron slapped a hand over my mouth before I could scream. The hand grasping me yanked me backwards and sat me back down in my chair. I tried to wriggle around to see who it was, but they wouldn't let me.

"Stop struggling, sweet," a voice commanded.

I stopped abruptly, and they let me turn around. A young man was standing above me, still holding tight to my arm. Cameron and Marc were staring up at him, and neither knew what to say. I wished they would find their voices soon to release me. But they still didn't move. The guy had tangled brown hair that fell to his shoulders, and a funny half-smile half-sneer. It was kind of creepy. His jacket bulged in all places, and when he shifted to get a better hold of me, I saw him flex his muscles.

"Let go!" I said quietly, trying to sound brave. I hoped it worked. But the smile-sneer man just smiled-sneered more.

"Not yet," he laughed. Finally, when at last I thought my arm would fall off, or my blood flow had completely stopped, he let go. I cradled my arm, and Marc and Cameron stood over me protectively.

"What was that for?" Cameron asked accusingly, and glanced around to be sure the man had nothing to do with his father.

"I needed to talk to her. Well, to all of you," the man explained. He offered his hand, but I felt like biting it instead of shaking it. Instead, I did neither. I gave him my best glare yet. He laughed some more, and let his hand drop. "The name's Tino. And who are you?" he asked.

"Nobody in particular," I answered defiantly.

"Right," Cameron backed me up.

"Like I'm going to believe that." Tino crossed his arms over his chest and looked us up and down. He sighed, and licked his lips. He glanced at me, then Cameron, and let his gaze linger on Marc. "Don't even think about escaping, alright? I know every nook and cranny in this stinking

airport, and if I have to, I'll run into the ladies room to catch
'ya."

That guy scared me. He was serious. But my curiosity
won over my fear and made me think - was that the guy
Griffin had contacted over the walkie-talkie? Was Tino
waiting for him right then? Should we try to escape? Tino
had said so himself - we shouldn't. But we had to if we
wanted to get away with our scheme. The only thing I could
think to do would be to distract him, and make a run for it.
We wouldn't hide - he'd only find us - we'd run straight to a
tour bus and go back to Cameron's house. But for some
reason, I didn't think that was going to happen.

"Do you like riddles?" Tino asked abruptly, interrupting
my planning. Before we had a chance to answer, he said, "I
know you're all thinking the same thing. And the answer is
yes. I am the one Griffin contacted. Another question you're
thinking: Is he on his way now? The answer is no. I like to
have a little fun with my victims before I turn them in, so
here's the deal: You answer all of my riddles correctly, and
I'll let you go. No mention of you to Griffin at all. My word
of honor. But if you answer wrong, you're all Griffin's. He
can do what he likes with you. I don't care. What do you
say?"

We looked at each other. Did we really have a choice? It
was worth a try. We shook our heads 'yes' and Tino smiled.

"Here we go. First riddle:

Liar, liar, pants on fire.

I know your situations dire.

If you don't admit I will explode

so hurry up and crack this code.

I'm waiting.

I'm counting out the beats

of your frightened little hearts
1, 2, 3, don't you just want to depart?
If you show me what you've got,
which I know is quite a lot,
maybe then I will not spill...
or kill.
What am I?"

Marc and Cameron put their heads together and began to whisper. I just laughed. Was that guy serious? The riddle was easy! The answer was in the third line!

"A bomb," I answered, and made sure there was no dirt in my fingernails. That stuff could really get stuck in there...and then you had to cut them and clean them to get it out...gross.

"Creed! Are you sure?" Marc cried. I knew what he was wondering. Had I just ruined our chance? But I knew I hadn't. I would've talked to him and Cameron about it if I hadn't been so sure.

I could feel the boys' eyes boring into me from behind. I continued to scrutinize my fingernails.

"How...how did you know?" Tino stammered. Apparently not many people had solved that particular riddle. I couldn't really figure out why.

"Tino...you'll have to do better than that. It was so ridiculously easy." I settled back in my chair and leaned my feet on the table. Tino just continued to stare at me and finally, after several minutes of thinking and Cameron and Marc whooping, he took a deep breath and said,

"Fine. Here's two more: A man was to be sentenced, and the judge told him, 'You may make a statement. If it is true, I'll sentence you to four years in prison. If it is false, I'll sentence you to six years in prison.' After the man made his statement, the judge decided to let him go free. What did the man say?" he paused, then continued on with the second riddle, "What's broken every time it's spoken?"

I tried to be polite while waiting for Tino to finish. Then, just as I opened my mouth, Marc grabbed my arm.

"Let's talk about these, okay?" I rolled my eyes and turned to look at them.

"Come on guys! You can't be serious! Let me answer these; they're easy. Easier than the first one."

"Fine," Cameron surprised Marc by saying. He pulled him back a step and whispered something in his ear. Marc smiled and looked relieved, but didn't say anything. I really didn't care...for once. I was itching to answer the riddles and get them right.

"Here's the answer to the first one. The guy said: 'You'll sentence me to six years in prison,' because if it was true, the judge would have had to make it false by sentencing him to four years in prison. And if it was false, he would've had to give him six years, which would make it true. So instead of contradicting his word, the judge decided to let him go. The answer to the second one is 'silence'."

Tino swore under his breath and grumbled,

"If you thought those were easy...try this one. I made it up myself and it's almost impossible to figure out."

"Try me."

"All right. Here it is:

> Holding you in their clutch
> is what they want so much
> with freedom in the distance
> and the ropes binding you
> you have some choices - only two.
> Pick one and keep watching it

pick two and cross over it
feel them in your mouth
on the tip of you tongue
when you give them, too.
What are they?"

I yawned. Tino smiled triumphantly, expecting me to give him the wrong answer.

"Rules," I answered lazily. I couldn't understand why Tino couldn't do any better.

"WHAT?!" he cried. "Not one person I've ever told that to has gotten it! No one! And I've told many people!"

We were silent. He watched me for a moment before we heard a sudden sound.

"Reese? Yes, I checked it out. I know the damage is bad. But I want that girl Julia fired, understood? She's of no use to this airport, believe me." Only one person I knew had that voice. And his name was Griffin.

None of us could move for the time being.

"Go!" Tino whispered. "I gave you my word! Go, now! You got all of them right; you deserve this. But if I spot you again - I'm turning you in." We nodded, and Cameron and Marc whisked me away. We didn't even stop to listen to the conversation Griffin had with Tino. Actually, I didn't really want to hear it anyway. I didn't want to even imagine it.

We reached the bus just as it was about to leave. There were more passengers than last time, probably because most had just unloaded from a plane. We sat down wearily and looked around, just in case Tino had betrayed us and Griffin sent a spy after us. You never know. One thing I've learned: You can't trust anyone.

I kept thinking about the riddles all the way back. Thankfully, Marc and Cameron kept silent except for a few occasional whispers. I was glad because I didn't want them asking me any questions about the easy riddles. They wouldn't believe me if I said they were easy, which they were, so there was no point in explaining.

Obviously, they really wanted to talk to me about it but were restraining for my sake. Finally, when they couldn't bear it any longer, they popped the question. "Creed - how did you know those answers?"

For some reason, I had a slight feeling that they weren't expecting any good answer. Nor did they need one or want one.

"I don't know," I answered, and continued looking out the window.

"You don't?" Marc asked, surprised.

"NO," I answered truthfully. Did *they* know why? If so, why were they asking me? Sometimes, I wished people would just come and out say what they wanted to say.

"You don't realize...you really don't know?" Cameron asked, perplexed.

"NOOOOOO," I answered, and gave them an annoyed look. They stopped pestering me for a couple of minutes before they continued.

"Creed - look at me," Cameron instructed. I didn't want to do what he asked, but I was genuinely curious, so I looked. He was looking at me fixedly, his eyes narrowed, with a slight smile on his face. "What am I feeling?" he asked. I wondered if he was trying to hypnotize me.

"You're feeling confused; slightly; you want to know all there is to know about my talent and Marc's, you're relieved in a way, awed by my presence and by Marc's, and a little intimidated because you had no idea how I was going to answer," I said this so quickly I wasn't even sure if I had really said it. I clapped my hand over my mouth as soon as the words escaped it. Where had that come from? What did I mean by 'my talent' and how on earth had I known that? Suddenly, I was the one feeling confused. I decided to try it on Marc. I could read his expression as if it were an open book with his feelings printed in large letters across the page.

His eyes were large, with admiration and respect glinting in them. His smile was like a congratulations, like 'you did it!' or 'aren't you proud?' He looked as if he could laugh out loud. But there was something else; a cloud, a shadow; lingering over his expression. There was concern and worry in his eyes, hidden behind his other feelings.

"What are you, Creed?" Cameron asked with a pinch of excitement in his voice.

"A Puzzler," I answered promptly. Then I understood. The page from Cecily's journal flashed across my mind, and I smiled. So I could solve any riddle; no sweat; and I could understand basically everything anyone said to me. I could tell what they were really feeling at all times, too. Like I had just done with Marc. But then I realized something more. (I had a feeling I'd be experiencing realization a lot more in the future.) I'd really been understanding and knowing Marc's feelings for my whole life. I guess it just took stages to reach the real point at which you know what you are.

"You get it now?" Marc whispered when Cameron wasn't looking. I knew exactly what he meant. Of course I got it. I totally understood how Marc had felt when he'd learned all about Communicators. Now I had the same feeling, bubbling up inside of me and wanting so desperately to share it with everyone around.

I was a Puzzler.

Eagle Eye

Helen had taken to standing out on her balcony at least once a day. She was watching, watching with the eye of a hawk. She didn't know what she was hoping, yet she carried the hope in her heart, hidden away in a small pouch that hung in her chest - hiding. Maybe she was hoping for her mother to come appearing over the sunset in the distance, to give her advice and to reign over Pastel again. Helen had no doubt that Ryn would be a good Queen, but she couldn't help wondering if Ryn could stand the pressure - the constant stress and strain. Her father had dealt with it, and he was lazy. If Ryn was really going to do more than King Doulc, she would definitely experience a new level of the stress.

And she would lean on Helen, her younger sister, to help her through it all. Helen wasn't even Queen and she already felt a big burden. She didn't believe in herself.

Perhaps she was hoping that a message would appear to her in the sky, advice, words of wisdom - anything. But she knew that what she was really hoping for was to see Creed come back. From all that the girl's parents had told her, Creed was pretty magnificent. That was another thing Helen often did. When she wanted to be alone, and away from Katheryn's questions, she would steal away to Mr. and Mrs. Skye's quarters. No, she was not alone there, but it felt like it. Two people were much easier to be around than the many she had to deal with when spending time with Katheryn. Katheryn was always swarmed by city people, servants, maids, advisors, butlers, scientists, inventors, and, on top of it all, those annoying entertainers that stuck to her side like flies on flypaper.

She didn't understand why her father hadn't gotten rid of them. He had hated them, but they were something to complain about, so he kept them all the same. He ordered them around and made them do silly tricks. They didn't quite understand, that, being Doulc's daughters, Helen and Katheryn didn't like everything Doulc had. So they continued to show off in their stretchy, old-timey costumes. So Helen had taken to sending them off on hard, long errands that often left them tired and ready for bed. It wasn't necessarily abuse, they liked working for the Queen and her sister, but it was pretty close. Helen tried to think of it as "getting them out of her hair for a change."

At least Mr. and Mrs. Skye seemed to understand what the two orphaned girls wanted. They knew when they wanted to talk and could tell when they wanted to be alone. Privately, Helen considered herself their second daughter. She even felt a small connection to Creed, whom she knew nothing about. All she could gather about the girl were from the Skye's tales.

"She's curious. Almost every adjective beginning with 'c,'" Mrs. Skye laughed. "Confident, courageous, charismatic, charming, captivating, sometimes careless...and not to mention cute. She's...well, how else can I describe her other than saying she's just: Creed! Wonderful, amazing, impressive Creed."

"She does sound amazing," Helen said quietly. She didn't want to ruin the moment. Mr. and Mrs. Skye seemed to glow when they talked about Creed, and they looked so caught up in what they were saying. It was obvious they really loved their daughter. Creed was a lucky girl.

When Helen wasn't spending time with Mr. and Mrs. Skye, she was spending time with Stella.

She often said, "Stella, can I talk to you?"

"Yes," was the constant reply. It was reassuring to let your worries free, to get them off your chest. Helen was able to do this when she talked to Mr. and Mrs. Skye and Stella. She talked to Stella about more personal matters. She did so more often now, because Ryn was off ruling the city. She might stare off into space and whisper, "This was mother's favorite room in the palace," or "Did you know that father was once actually a wonderful King? He turned to the dark side after mother died." Helen usually avoided the topic of her mother, but there were times when she just couldn't resist talking about her. She missed her so much.

If only Creed would come back. But the thing was this: What if Creed was the wrong person to put so much hope in? Would Creed let her down if she ever came back? For the moment, those questions were left unanswered.

◆ ◆ ◆

Spying

Griffin wasn't home when we returned, just as we had expected. We changed clothes so he wouldn't be able to identify us when he got back. We told Ben we'd gone to visit the Trevi Fountain and some other wonders of Rome. He didn't believe us. Well, at least Marc and Cameron thought he believed us, but I didn't. I could see right through him. He was suspicious of us. Even though we had quite convincingly told him there was nothing to worry about. Anyways...we would need to be careful.

I told Cameron he'd better not look guilty at dinner, and he just reddened. I rolled my eyes and told him to wear some blush or something. He just reddened even more.

Marc described in detail all of the damage he had done to the plane, and we praised him highly. Neither of us could have done such a good job. Cameron's conscience would've gotten in the way first, and I wouldn't even have known where to begin. I was smart, but I wasn't *that* smart.

We laughed when we remembered how I had called Cameron 'mute' when Griffin arrived on the scene. We laughed about Julia and her bob and her pink fingernails. I told them how I had heard Griffin fire her, and we talked some more about our successful adventure.

Just then, we heard a door slam and rough footsteps. They advanced towards Cameron's room. Immediately, we changed subjects and began talking about the gelato we had had on our trip into Rome.

"CAMERON!" a voice boomed. "I need you. NOW." It was right outside the door. Then came a knock. It was so hard I thought the wood would splinter. Cameron gulped, but held his chin up high and walked slowly to the door. He opened it, and Griffin beckoned for him to follow. Then Griffin slammed the door in our faces. I knew he could have a...how do you say it?...bad side...but I didn't know he could act like that. He must have been really mad. I hoped he hadn't figured out it was us. If Tino had slipped...Cameron would get into so much trouble.

Marc and I waited for the footsteps to recede, then followed the sounds of loud voices down the hallway. We stopped at the door to Griffin's room.

"Cameron! I can't believe this!" We could hear Griffin pacing. Every time he neared the door we jumped back. "Why would you do something like this?" he asked. So he did know.

"What are you talking about?" I let out a pent up breath. Cameron hadn't given up yet. I could almost picture him: chest out proudly, dark hair falling across his eyes, his hand pushing it back and the deep blue eyes giving a message of their own; a proud, confident message.

"I'm talking about my plane!" Griffin cried, then groaned.

"Dad! What happened to your plane?" Cameron's voice was filled with fake concern. Good. He was playing it cool.

"As if you don't know! I'm almost sure it was some of your genius friends who did it! The plane is basically unrepairable."

Marc grinned at that comment. Without knowing it, Griffin had just called Marc a genius.

"Oh my gosh! Dad, I'm so sorry! I had no idea! I promise you - neither my friends or I were behind this! Do you really think I'd do something like that to tear you down? I know how much this means to you!"

Marc and I gave each other silent high fives. Cameron was playing his part perfectly. He sounded hurt...as if his dad had insulted him by even suggesting that he and his friends had sabotaged the plane.

"Look...I'm sorry, Cameron. I didn't mean to hurt you, or anything. It's just...I'm really upset, and I thought you didn't want this...so, I thought...you know, maybe it was you."

"I'm sorry, too, Dad," Cameron paused, then hurriedly said, "For the plane. I'm sorry that happened to the plane." We heard Griffin give Cameron a hug, and then they began advancing to the door. We hurried to our rooms, and were just in time to flop down on the beds and open Marc's book when Cameron walked in. He looked really upset.

I tried to talk to him, but he'd only answer with, "Not now, Creed."

It took a couple of hours before he was really ready to talk. He admitted he was a little upset for doing what we did to his dad, but he reminded himself that he didn't believe in what his dad wanted, so what was done was done. There was no turning back. I felt bad for him, but what else could I say? I hadn't ever sabotaged anything before.

Cameron and Griffin were pretty quiet at dinner, though both tried to make pleasant conversation. Marc and Ben didn't even realize they were still distressed, but I knew those things. Andria was still in her room, sleeping.

Cameron had to bring dinner to her on a tray. Griffin told us she should be due soon.

I knew it was a bit selfish, but I really wanted her to hurry up and have the baby. It would keep Griffin from going anywhere...like, say, to find Scharr or possibly even Pastel.

I was so excited when dinner finally ended, although by that time, Griffin was looking exceedingly better. Little did I know, things were going to start picking up pace. It was the last time I would see Ben for a while, and the beginning of my times with Griffin.

I had a feeling I knew why he looked so happy...but I'd need more than just one person to check it out. I decided to recruit none other than the wonderful (literally) Cameron, and the brilliant Marc. I told them my plan, and we got right to work.

Cameron was stationed in his very own room. (genius - I know.) Griffin and Andria's room was backed up to it, and Cameron might be able to hear something important. Marc was stationed outside their room, and I had the most dangerous location of all...I was to be in the room. Yes, I was planning to hide under the bed, or in the closet, or behind the desk...somewhere.

I had Cameron distract his dad, and luckily, his mom was asleep. I tiptoed in, and Cameron and Marc made an excuse for me saying I was napping. It wasn't a bad excuse...Ben and Griffin still thought I was pretty sick.

They had Griffin trapped in the kitchen when I slipped into the room. It was spacious, with big windows on the far wall and bookshelves lining the other. The bed faced the shelves, and the closet was next to the bed by the windows.

Andria lay resting in the bed, sound asleep and oblivious to the world around her. She reminded me so much of my mom for a moment that I wanted to go lay down next to her...touch her arm, give her a hug. But I restrained. Her husband was the one causing me so much trouble. I glanced around me for a moment, eager to soak it all up while I was there.

The bedspread was a burnt orange, a beautiful color for living in a city like Rome. There was an elaborate painting above the bed, a copy of a painting from the ceiling of the Sistine Chapel. It was so entrancing...so beautiful...that I barely noticed the footsteps approaching. They weren't Cameron's...nor Marc's nor Ben's...and there was only one person left in the house who the footsteps could belong to. Griffin. Hiding under the desk would've been too noticeable...but behind the desk wasn't. It backed up against the wall...but there was plenty of space for me to hide. A plant sat at the end of the desk, so if Griffin happened to look at my hiding spot, the plant would be blocking the view. Perfect. I crawled behind it just in time, and lay down flat on my stomach. It wouldn't work if I couldn't see anything, but luckily there was a hole in the middle open shelf. It was supposed to be for cords and such, but Griffin hadn't yet put any there, so it made a perfect peep hole.

Griffin walked into the room and sat down on the bed. He looked at his wife for a moment, then crossed over to the desk. He came closer and closer and closer...and then I couldn't see any more. I shut my eyes tight and pressed my body against the desk so Griffin couldn't see me if he leaned over. At least, I hoped he wouldn't. I heard him pick something up and press a couple of buttons. The phone. He had picked up the phone.

He grunted when no one answered, and re-dialed. Again, no answer. I wondered who he was calling. I could feel his impatience as he sat down and logged onto his computer. I had stared at it for a moment when I went in...it was a really nice Apple laptop, silver and white that glittered when the sun shone down on it from the window. I heard him type something in, a password maybe, and then he clicked into something.

"AH HAH!" he cried and clicked away again. He clicked clicked clicked for so long that I wondered if hiding behind his desk had been a bad idea. What if I didn't pick up any clue as to what he was planning next? I was sure he was planning something...that was certain. I could feel it in my bones. Plus, if I were Griffin, I'd do anything to get my way if it really meant that much to me. Although there was one thing Griffin didn't know...we would too.

Griffin stopped typing abruptly and picked up the phone again. He plopped down next to his wife and dialed for the third time. I saw him cross his fingers and bite his lip. That time, someone answered.

"Adam!" he laughed, relieved, before continuing. "Hey man...what's up?" He smiled as he listened to Adam on the other end of the line. "Yeah...well, I've come across a small problem. What? Yes, I am. I want to take you up on your offer, if you don't mind....mmmm...alright. Yeah, I thought about that too...but I don't have a choice! The plane was sabotaged by some rowdy kids this morning, and I have no idea what to do about it. Then I remembered you...yes, exactly! You get it! Thanks so much! Yes, I want to get it done as quickly as possible. How about tomorrow morning...I don't want to take any chances. Yeah...I'm afraid we're being watched. But no one except my family knows about you, so I think we're good. Alright! See you tomorrow. Be ready for the trip of your life, Adam!"

Griffin hung up and danced around the room, obviously excited. I knew why. He was getting his 'trip of a lifetime' after all. Ugghhh! Why hadn't Cameron told us about that offer? Marc could've sabotaged that plane, too! I wondered if he was on his father's side after all. And to think I'd liked him at all. Whatever. Appearances didn't mean everything.

As soon as Griffin left the room, I hurried out. I was ready to give Cameron a piece of my mind.

Little did I know, as I left, a pen fell to the floor.

Kidnapped

Griffin was in the kitchen eating a snack, giddy with glee. I couldn't believe it. If we went out, we'd probably be caught. We were definitely in a predicament. The only thing we could do was plead Griffin not to go. Beg him...entreat him...get down on our knees or throw tantrums...anything to keep him from going.

I met Marc out in the hall. He was pacing up and down very impatiently.

"How did it go?" Marc asked as soon as we had ducked into my room. I snuggled under the covers and tried to appear as if I had just woken up from a nap.

"It...it was good...but not good," I said, and looked out the window.

"What do you mean?" Marc asked worriedly, casting a glance at the door.

"Griffin's got a backup. And I think Cameron knew about it all along. Some guy named Adam has another plane, and apparently Griffin chose to use the other one instead of Adam's. I think Griffin was expecting someone to sabotage the plane, so he acted like the one at the airport was really the one he was going to use. Now that someone *has* sabotaged the plane, he's going to pretend like he can't go, when he's actually going to use Adam's...which I suspect is better."

"But...but you can't be serious! Cameron helped us!"

"I know...but I bet Griffin told Cameron to act like he wanted to help us. If we wanted to sabotage the plane, Cameron was to make sure it happened - and then act like we had accomplished everything and we had saved the day. Then Griffin, in secret, could leave in Adam's plane."

"Creed! It just sounds too farfetched. Besides, he even agreed to let you go into his parent's room to spy on them."

"Ummm..." I looked at Marc guiltily. I had a confession to make. "Well - I told Cameron I was hiding in the living room, on the other side of his parent's room. I was afraid he wouldn't let me go in there." Marc stared at me.

"Creed!" Even though Marc was still jealous of Cameron, and had probably been desperate for Cameron to mess up at something, he had still trusted him and wanted to trust him. I did too. I really liked Cameron. Well, Marc and I both knew. You couldn't let emotions get in your way.

We talked for a little while longer, discussing what we should do, when Cameron arrived at to the door. He burst in and went over to sit with us. I shrugged away. He looked at me strangely, then asked,

"What happened? What did you guys find out? There's too much insulation in the walls for me to hear anything," He turned to me. "So you probably didn't find much out, either, huh?"

"Uhhhhhh...no. Nothing. Only the fact that you're a TRAITOR!" I couldn't help myself. I was supposed to act like I had found out nothing, so that Cameron wouldn't go and report to his father. Like father like son.

"WHAT? Where...what...how? I'm not a traitor!" Cameron jumped off the bed and looked me straight in the eye.

"Yes you are!" I accused. "You're working with your father...you don't want to help us!" I glared at him until my eyes got moist and I felt like I could cry. What else could go wrong? Hadn't I endured enough already?

"Why do you think that?" Cameron asked quietly. He shook his head and looked away. "I'm not like Griffin," he whispered hoarsely. I could feel the agony pulsing through his veins. But I refused to believe he really felt that way.

"Because! Griffin has a backup plan! And you knew all about it - you just didn't choose to tell us about it! Why? Because I'm right! You're a traitor, and you know it!"

Cameron turned to look at me so harshly I gulped. He narrowed his eyes and pressed his lips into a thin line. Marc scooted over to me, but I barely noticed. It was between me and Cameron. He was as pale as a ghost...not red with anger like before. He rubbed his hand over his face and groaned, long and slow...almost painfully.

"Creed. Marc. I'm sorry if you think I'm a traitor...but I'm not. You're wrong," he said slowly, with great deliberation. Then his voice got rougher - angrier. "If you want to think that...go right ahead! You know, I don't care! I did all of this for you! And you know what - I wish you had *never* come!" He glared at us for one last second before storming out the door...and running smack into Griffin.

"What's this?" Griffin asked sweetly. "Having a fight already? But you barely know each other!" He held up the pen from his desk. I sucked in my breath.

I backed up...inch by inch until I was practically in Marc's arms. Cameron was staring at Griffin, wide-eyed. Griffin stared back, with the same smile Tino had worn when we had first met him.

"You got away with your little scheme once, kids, but it's not going to happen again. I intend to take over now. I may not be as bad as your regular kidnapper...I mean, I've gotten to know you guys. I've taken a liking to you. And Cameron, you're my son. I love you with all my heart. I'm actually quite sorry I'm going to do this...but you guys know too much and I'm afraid you're going to try to sabotage me again. Plus, I have a feeling that two of you know more than you'll admit."

Griffin smiled, and before Cameron could bolt out the door, he backed up against it and locked it shut. I got a sick feeling in my stomach. I took one look in Griffin's eyes and saw pools of emotions in them...emotions too overwhelming and deep for me. I was only going through the first few stages of being a Puzzler, after all!

I could feel Marc's breath against my neck - that was how close he was. He reached down and squeezed my hand. I felt the color drain from my face. So many thoughts were running through my head. Griffin had a backup...Cameron wasn't a traitor...Ben seemed so far away; too oblivious to save us...Griffin was kidnapping us...and his emotions were so strong they seemed to be coursing through me, as well. That's when I blacked out.

♦ ♦ ♦

Cameron had been too upset to even hear the approaching footsteps...to hear them stop in front of the door. He hadn't even thought to lower his voice. He was so mad at himself. Terribly mad. He felt even worse when he glanced back at Creed. She was so pale...and looked so fragile...that was because she was. He could tell she was dealing with tremendous strain. Then he realized. He'd read about it in Cecily's journal. Again, she had resorted to describing Puzzlers, Communicators, the Analytical type...and he remembered one short passage where she had described the one thing young Puzzlers couldn't deal with...too much emotion. He looked over at Griffin. He wasn't a Puzzler...but he could definitely tell there were too many emotions going through him. Poor Creed. He turned around once more...just in time to see her collapse into Marc's arms, limp. He ran over to help Marc, who looked like he could black out, too. It was all his fault. If only he had convinced his dad from sending up the plane. Then they wouldn't be in the whole mess.

Together, Cameron and Marc eased Creed onto the bed. Her hair fell around her face, which was dotted with perspiration. Her eyes were closed, and she looked pale as a ghost. Cameron groaned. That was the last thing Creed needed...to get sick again.

"Alright! Let's wrap this up. Cameron, Marc, grab Creed and escort her out the window. At least try to get her to the car."

Cameron, who was older and therefore stronger than Marc, lifted Creed off the bed and wrapped her in his arms. She was as light as a feather, probably under 100 pounds...underweight for a 13 year old. Griffin opened the window and stepped out before them to help them out. Cameron went next, and Griffin, who wasn't necessarily the best at being an evil kidnapper, helped carry Creed. Marc came last, hiding his and Creed's packs under his shirt. Griffin barely noticed. Silent as mice, they tiptoed through the shrubs to the back of the house to get Griffin's car. He stowed them inside before starting the engine and locking the doors and windows.

Creed remained unconscious for most of the ride, which was probably better for her since she would be too frightened if she were awake. She was brave, braver than any girl Cameron had ever known, but she was still only 13...and there was a limit to the things she could handle.

"Alright. Because I just can't possibly wait until morning, I figured it would be best to go straight to the airport. Or, actually, to Adam's house. He lives right next door to the airport, and once dawn breaks, we can go straight there and head off." He laughed, and looked back at the three kids. "I'm taking all of you with me," he cackled. Then he said soberly, "Guys...I really am sorry for this. It may not seem like it, but I...you guys are so great, and don't think of this as a kidnapping."

Griffin looked Cameron in the eyes, and pulled off the road.

"I just want to take you guys with me so you don't get into any trouble." He looked up at the sky, then declared, "Yes, that's right. I just want to make sure you guys don't get into any trouble while I'm away." That seemed to improve his conscience, so the boys didn't say anything. They guessed he was right. Griffin wouldn't really kidnap them. After all, if he was taking them with him, and he wasn't going anywhere illegal, was it really kidnapping?

"Yes, it is!" Marc whispered in Portuguese, one language Griffin didn't know. "He took us against our will!"

"But all parents can do that....they're parents!"

"He's not my dad! Or Creed's!"

"Fine. But...he's not tying us up or anything, right? And he's being nice...right?"

"I guess so." Marc looked into Cameron's eyes and could guess what he was thinking. "I'm not going to report him for this, Cameron. We're trying to stay low key, remember? Besides, Griffin is a friend. He's helped us come this far, hasn't he?" Cameron looked at Marc gratefully. Marc continued. "Besides, what if he's really doing us a favor now? Creed and I have to get home at some point, don't we?"

Cameron was so surprised at what Marc had just said that he almost forgot to comment.

"WHAT? How...but you haven't even found Creed's journal yet! And how will you get there without my dad finding Scharr? What about Cecily? What about *me*?"

"Cameron! Calm down!" Marc sighed and looked out the window, trying to find a way to answer Cameron. He looked down at Creed; she would know what to do. She was a Puzzler, after all. He was only a Communicator. "Cameron, I know we haven't found the journal yet; but we can't stay here Below for the rest of our lives searching for a needle in a haystack! No, a speck in a haystack. It's that unlikely. I have a theory on getting to Pastel without your dad finding either it or Scharr...but I'm trying to think it over first. I have no idea what to do about Cecily. Have you ever wondered whether or not what she was saying was true? Or was she just writing some fantasy because she despised her father?"

Cameron reddened. He had considered that possibility, hundreds of times. But something about Cecily...something about her personality that just popped off the page...something about the words she wrote and the evidence she had...he hated to believe it was all a lie. If only he had found Creed's journal instead. No...he wished he hadn't found either of them. Or if he did, he should have just left it where he found it, and when Creed and Marc came, he could've just told them where he'd found one.

"And you? I'm not worried about you. You've got a very successful life ahead of you." It was Marc's turn to redden as he said this. He looked down at his fingers, and began to entwine them. It kept him busy, and he wouldn't have to look at Cameron.

"Thanks, Marc. But I don't care about the successful future I have right now. I'm all about exploring new roads...new places, new people." Marc looked up when he said this and smiled. "If you guys can't find that journal, I'll find it for you."

Marc couldn't believe what he was hearing. He looked up incredulously.

"No way!"

"Way."

The two boys clapped hands and laughed before switching back to English.

♦ ♦ ♦

I yawned and stretched. I felt much better, filled with strength and energy. I looked around. We were in a car; I assumed it was Griffin's; and Cameron, Marc, and I were sitting in the back seat. The seats were leathery and warm. The car felt stuffy, even though Griffin had already rolled down all the windows. Marc and Cameron were jabbering on about something, and I presumed they had just finished talking in another language. They couldn't seem to lose the accent or speed after talking in a different launguage for at least ten minutes. Funny; I know, but true. They seemed to notice me for the first time when I sat up. Marc looked worried, but Cameron didn't. That bugged me. He was supposed to be worried about me...frantic that I had passed out...anxious as to whether or not I might die...alright, alright, that may have been a little dramatic. But, still. He was supposed to look upset.

"Got overwhelmed?" he asked, and his eyes sparkled. I knew exactly what he was talking about...Griffin's emotions...but how had he known? Then I remembered Cecily's journal. He had read the whole thing; there was bound to be more information about Puzzlers in it. If only I had remembered to bring it so I could read the rest. Darn.

Marc looked at Cameron strangely, and soon they were off on some conversation in some Chinese language. I knew Cameron was explaining to Marc what he meant by 'got overwhelmed?' but I still wanted to understand the words. You'd think, being a Puzzler, I could figure out what they were saying, but that would be stretching things, I guess. I couldn't be a Superhero and save the world, unfortunately. Let me re-phrase that: I can't be a Superhero and save Scharr, unfortunately.

I let Cameron switch places with me, and was soon staring out the window at the surrounding beauty of Rome. At the time, I had no idea what might come next - and what it would mean for my future.

I knew we might never see Rome again. Or we would escape and hurry back to Griffin's house to get Ben and leave. We might never see Ben again...or Andria, or Cameron. And what would happen to him? Would we just leave him behind Down Below and hope to forget about him? I didn't think I could do that. He was implanted in my memory. Thinking of Cameron reminded me of Cecily. What would happen to her? Would she live in Scharr for the rest of her life and never be freed from the wrath of Elias, O Evil One? She sounded as if she had lived a similar life, and I couldn't bear to think about it. I knew what it felt like...shouldn't we help her? And the biggest question of all, was, of course, where was *my* journal? We had found a journal. From another person living in the sky. But it wasn't *mine*. The whole point of the journey had been to find my precious journal. Heck - we had traveled down through the Alps, past Florence, through the Apennines, all the way to Rome! We had done a pretty magnificent job, and yet I couldn't help thinking that it had all been in vain.

A while later, Cameron told Marc and I about the people we were going to see. He mentioned a girl named Fabia, so I asked, "Who's she?"

"Adam's daughter," he explained. Then, "Adam isn't Italian...he met Eloisa, his wife, here in Rome and they fell in love. Now they've got Fabia. She's part English and part Italian."

"I like her name!" Once he was done describing the family, I leaned against the window and stared out at all of the passing scenery.

Hills ran past the window. The cool air tunneled into my face, whipping my hair in every way. I leaned back and relaxed. I probably wouldn't be able to do that again. I wondered what lay ahead.

◆ ◆ ◆

The Pawn Shop

Fabia stretched her neck and tucked her legs underneath her to make herself higher. Why did the backseats of cars have to be so low? That car ride was worth it, though. She was sure of that much. She may have been only 6, but she understood more than people thought she did. For instance, she had understood what a pawn shop was as soon as her mother had explained it. Pawn shops were places where you could buy stuff for cheap, and sell stuff you didn't need. She liked those kinds of places, considering she only got 25 cents a week for allowance. She had been saving up, and she had $5.25. Her mother said it was probably enough to buy something small, and that was all that mattered to Fabia. As long as she got something she could share with her friends.

She also wanted to look impressive. Fabia was a very regal child. She liked to look done-up, dressed in pretty dresses or skirts. She liked wearing her mother's jewelery and the big bows in her dark hair. Even her friends had said it looked nice.

Today, however, she needed to look impressive not just for fun, but for a very 'special' occasion, as her mother put it. Mr. Griffin, a friend of her daddy's, was going to stay at *her* house for a day or so. He was going to bring his son, Cameron. Fabia liked visitors, although they always exclaimed how cute she was or how tiny she was or how much she had grown. It grew really annoying, and after a while, Fabia had taken to acting shy and quiet. That was more her personality, but she did enjoy having long conversations with people.

"Look, Fabia! We're here! See that shop over there? The one with the big awning and windows?" Eloisa, her mother, pointed to small shop on the other side of the street. She parked the old family car and helped Fabia out. Fabia hated to admit it; but she was quite small - no matter how hard her family tried to convince her that 'she had gotten so big lately.' No. They couldn't fool her.

She hopped down and held her mother's hand as they crossed the street. It wasn't too busy; for there weren't too many cars around; and they arrived on the other side quickly. They followed another person into the shop, a man with tangled hair and disgusting breath. A beer bottle stuck out of his pocket, already empty. Fabia felt her mother's hand close tightly around her own. Her mother led her around the shop, and Fabia saw a lot of things she liked...but none particularly interesting. She spotted lamp shades, sheets, a mattress leaning against the wall, a jewelery dresser, a section devoted to light bulbs, old, tattered books, silverware, and more. But what Fabia found her eyes traveling to more and more frequently was the man who had entered the shop before them. He was leaning on the counter, talking quietly to the man behind it.

She pulled her mother closer and pretended to look at some books while the men talked.

"Do you have it?" The man behind the counter whispered.

"Of course I have it, you fool! Do your friends call you the village idiot? They should."

"Well, you could've forgotten it, and then look what situation we'd have been in! If you had to come any other day, the boss would probably be the one standing here, and you know he doesn't buy any stolen items!" Unfortunately, Fabia did not hear the 'stolen items' part. She was too busy wondering what a village idiot was. She knew she probably shouldn't ask her mother.

"Yes, yes, I know." The man dug around in his pocket a bit and pulled out something small. He handed it to the man behind the counter and he examined it thoroughly. When he held it up, it glinted in the sun shining through the windows. Once he took it out of the glare, Fabia finally realized what it was. A bracelet. A golden bracelet. Fabia wanted it at once.

"Mommy!" She pointed at it eagerly. Her mother turned and stared at the object the man was turning over in his palm.

"It's beautiful!" she whispered. Then she snapped out of it. "But it's probably much too expensive. I am not going to help you pay for it."

"Can I *please* see how much it is?" Fabia pleaded. She looked up at her mother with her big blue eyes and gave her the sad face. Eloisa glanced back and forth between her daughter and the bracelet. The men at the counter were still lost in conversation. Finally, Eloisa cast her daughter an annoyed look, but pulled her up to the counter all the same.

"Excuse me? My daughter wanted to know how much that bracelet's worth." The men looked at each other. With a sigh, the salesman looked at it and bit his lip. His answer was slow and deliberate. When the man announced the price, Eloisa almost fainted in astonishment. The man was practically *giving* her the bracelet, it was so cheap! The men obviously didn't realize that the bracelet was made of real gold! She bought the bracelet right away and slipped it onto Fabia's wrist. Fabia smiled in triumph. She loved the way the bracelet looked on her slim wrist, so shiny and golden and beautiful! Her mother grasped her hand and pulled her out of the store, for she was in such a dreamlike state that it was almost unbelievable.

When they got into the car, Fabia began thinking about where she wanted to put it when she got home. She had received a jewelery box for her 5th birthday, so she figured she'd place it in that for safe-keeping. But until then, she wanted to wear it and show it off with pride.

Fabia took it off, handling it as carefully as if it were glass, and examined it as thoroughly as the man behind the counter had. The bracelet really did catch the light; and when she looked at it's underside she was surprised to find a dull spot. When she looked closer, she realized it was a name, an engraved name in curly-cue letters. She could read; very well, actually; but tiny curly-cue letters were just not her thing. She reminded herself to get her mother to read it to her later.

The ride home was short when you had something to occupy yourself with, other than making yourself taller to look out the window. Fabia just couldn't seem to believe she really had the bracelet in her possession. She was beginning to think it wasn't really there, and had taken to touching it just to be sure, when her mother pulled into their driveway and Fabia was forced to go into the house. After showing her father, she changed into warmer attire and settled down to read. Sometimes her mother read to her, and sometimes she read by herself. Today she had to read by herself, for her mother was tidying the house for the visitors. And believe it or not, she actually forgot about the bracelet for the time being. Even when her father stepped through the door with the visitors...four, instead of two.

♦ ♦ ♦

Adam's Family

It was dark by the time we reached Adam's house. He was waiting out on the steps, turning something over and over again in his hands. Once we got closer, I could make out what it was: a disposable camera. You could probably find those all over Rome; considering it was one of the Below's hottest tourist spots.

Adam had bristly red hair, so bright it looked as if flames from a fire were covering his head. He had stubble on his chin, and his cheeks were ruddy. His blue eyes (odd for a red-head) glanced about and fell twice on me. I smiled, embarrassed. I wanted so badly to burst out laughing. Adam didn't fall into any stereotypes I knew. He seemed to be a mix of all of them. His red hair, bright eyes, and ruddy cheeks made him look country and southwestern. Yet his pressed khaki pants and brown polo made you wonder if he was rich or wealthy. His small wire glasses made him appear smart and sophisticated, and his tennis shoes looked sporty and new. He clapped Cameron on the shoulder and smiled at Marc and I.

"Hey, guys! What's up? Griffin! Haven't seen you in a while."

"I know! It's been...how long? Four or five years?"

"With only phone calls to fill in the time."

"Well, you look great! How are you feeling about tomorrow?" Griffin asked. He sounded a bit guilty to me...with a mix of excitement and anxiousness. I loved how I knew these things.

"I'm excited. That's why I've got the camera." He held it up for us to see and examined it himself. "Alright...enough talk...let's go inside. Eloisa and Fabia are waiting. Fabia is especially excited to see you guys, although she doesn't speak much English yet."

We walked up the steps of the big clay house and were ushered inside. Eloisa was standing in the doorway to the kitchen, her hands on the shoulders of young Fabia, who looked to be around 6 or 7.

"Ciao! Welcome to our home!" Eloisa cried. She rushed forward and embraced each of us. She had a slight Italian accent, probably because she'd been around Adam so long, but she definitely looked Italian. She had long, red-brown hair, and beautiful green eyes protected by long eyelashes. Fabia was beautiful, too, because she was half English and half Italian. She had the brown hair like her mother, wavy, and with dark bangs hanging over her forehead, but with the gorgeous blue eyes like her father. She had the same ruddy cheeks as him, all of his features, and her mother's figure.

"Ciao!" she said boldly. "I'm 6." She held up her fingers for us to see. I was almost right.

"Here, now. Let us find you guys a place to stay. Griffin, I know those two aren't your kids. Who are they?"

"These are Cameron's friends. They're...going on a trip with me."

"Ahhh...I see." Eloisa smiled, then took Fabia's hand and led her up the stairs. They were steep, and I kept watching Fabia to make sure she didn't fall. That was stupid, considering it was her house and she had probably climbed the stairs about a million times.

We reached the top, winded, and Eloisa smiled.

"Here is your room." She pointed to a small room right off the staircase. "It and this one..." She pointed to the one next to it. "...Are adjoining. I figured Creed and Marc could sleep in those. And Griffin, you can share the two-bed bedroom with Cameron." Eloisa smiled again and stroked Fabia's hair. Then she turned to me. "You will be right across the hall from Fabia."

Fabia looked up at me with those wide eyes of hers and giggled. It sounded like a nervous laugh...a sweet yet nervous laugh. I wondered if maybe she was a bit afraid of us.

Fabia and Eloisa soon left to give us time to unpack. My room was very small, but cozy and warm at the same time. The walls were a burnt orange, the bedspread blood red. The oak furniture gave it a really gorgeous look. I wanted badly to escape, so as I unpacked I thought of all the possible ways. The house was so tall that climbing out the window was insane. Trying to sneak out was insane, too.

Just as I was about to go nuts planning these things, Marc walked through our adjoining closet. It startled me at first, because he was suddenly just there when I turned around. I wondered how long he'd been watching me.

"Hey." He sat down on my bed and patted the spot next to him. Hesitantly, I stopped pacing and wringing my hands and sat down next to him. We sat there like that, neither knowing what to say. It was so embarrassing, all of a sudden. I didn't want to admit it - but it was getting harder and harder to have that intimate time together. Well, not exactly harder...but definitely embarrassing and uncomfortable. I found myself blushing every time.

"Hey," I finally said back.

"I don't have an escape plan." Marc looked away, then decided it was better to look at me straight in the eye. I could read his feelings plain on his face: Seriousness, sadness, anger, a bit of confusion...admiration. But that feeling was too little for me to really decipher.

"Why not?" I couldn't tear my eyes away. He held me locked in his gaze.

"Because I think it's time to go back," he whispered. This time he couldn't seem to bear looking at me. He turned his head.

"Go back? But why? I...my journal..." I croaked. What was he thinking? His plans were getting worse and worse by the day.

"We can't stay here forever, Creed." He reached over and took my hand. He was warm to the touch. I almost recoiled, then thought better of it. I wished he hadn't reminded me about going back. Actually, we really did have to stay Below forever. There was no way to get back up to Pastel without Griffin or someone else finding it. It made me sad - it made me dizzy with fright. I was so sad that I started crying. The tears just began to flow. The grief...the sadness...denial, hatred...it all came out again. I wondered how long it would take before I ran out of tears.

Marc tore his eyes away and got up from the bed to sit somewhere else. I could see his emotions, too, and he was toying with them like someone would a toy.

Nothing happened for at least ten minutes. Then Marc stood up and left. I wanted to stop sobbing, after all, Fabia was probably trying to sleep across the narrow hall. But something inside of me just had to let the tears flow on.

◆ ◆ ◆

The Illness

It had barely been a month before Katheryn fell ill. She tried to stay tough, tried not to let the weakness show through, but more and more people began to notice. The first to realize were the maids. Then the butlers and servants. By the second week of Katheryn's illness, practically everyone in the castle knew. Mr. and Mrs. Skye were getting well acquainted with Helen, and she told them about the sickness as soon as she found out..

It had started with a slight cold. It had been passed around; it was nothing to worry about. For a couple of days Katheryn suffered a bad headache, congestion, sore throat, and cough, and then she started getting drowsy just after lunch. She would lay down for a nap and wouldn't be able to wake up until later that evening, which caused her to feel awake when the sun went down and everyone else was going to bed. That passed soon enough; she just didn't take naps and made sure to get back to her regular schedule. Yet she was still severely tired almost all of the time, and after a week had passed she was confined to bed rest. The doctor came to take a look at her, and by that time she was showing signs of a low fever. It grew worse and worse as the days passed.

Now, Katheryn *had* inherited *some* stubbornness from her father, so she flat defied letting her advisors take over completely. She ordered that some of her work be brought to her in bed, and she let Helen read it to her as she closed her eyes and thought about it.

The doctor didn't want to tell Katheryn the illness; she would be too upset, but he did tell Helen, she being Katheryn's sister and everything.

Helen wept for days in the presence of Mr. and Mrs. Skye. If she broke down in front of her sister, it would only make her worse and a lot more worried. Helen didn't want to do that to Katheryn.

"I...I just don't want to upset her," she sniffed. Mrs. Skye brushed a tear away from her cheek and wrapped her arms around the girl.

"Everything is placed upon you, Helen! I'm so sorry! You should not have to carry such responsibility. You are only 14. That dumb doctor shouldn't have told you anything - even if you are Katheryn's younger sister! He should have only known how much it would upset you, too!"

Helen nodded. Everything did seem to be placed on her shoulders. She still had to watch the scientists down in the lab, make sure Katheryn's advisors weren't making any stupid decisions behind her back, take care of Katheryn herself, and give the maids, butlers, and servants their orders. She was reading Katheryn's paperwork out loud to her, taking the initiative to finish all of Katheryn's business...Mrs. Skye was right! Wasn't it a lot for one 14 year old? Although she was turning 15 soon, right after Katheryn turned 18. That was another thing she would be adding to her plate soon! A royal birthday for Her Highness. And she had been looking forward to that! Well, not anymore. For she was going to be the one planning it.

♦ ♦ ♦

Jump

Unlike my many quick nights, that one seemed to drag on. There was nothing I could do but stare out the window at the dark sky, wondering if back home everything was all right. Finally, morning arrived, and the sky glowed pink and purple when I glanced at it. Marc noticed my glance and smiled. I think he was trying to cheer me up about going home. Nothing seemed to cheer me up anymore...not even Marc.

Fabia tugged on my hand several times that morning, even though it was so early she probably could've gotten another two hours of sleep, and each time I answered, "Not now, Fabia. Maybe later." That was when she got the idea to tell me that it was "later" time. All I wanted was for her to go away, but I didn't want to hurt her feelings. So I played a quick game with her, knowing it was really time to go and Griffin would save me from that torture. It was funny - thinking like that - because Griffin was really doing nothing to save me at all. In fact, he was making matters worse. It was time to go up. Griffin was ready for "the trip of a life time" so quickly.

The ride to the airport was bumpy, so bumpy that I almost got car sick. Marc looked even more apprehensive, and Cameron just looked sad.

We arrived at dawn. The sun was just beginning to peek up at us over those big fluffy clouds that I knew held up my home. It was hard to believe we were really on our way back. Maybe home really would offer some relief...even though I still had to face King Doulc. But I couldn't help thinking...we'd gotten so far already, why not take down the King while we were at it?

The receptionist noticed us as soon as we walked in. She stood up out of respect and shook hands with Griffin and Adam both.

"My name is Marla. Nice to finally meet you, Mr. Griffin. I'm so glad you could find another plane in time. We're very upset about what happened to the other one." Her voice was sharp. That lady was definitely a professional, unlike Julia. She smiled and pushed her glasses farther up her nose. She was so thin and bony that they had been sliding down. With her long fingers (and clear - not pink - fingernails) she dialed a number with the phone sitting on her desk.

"Mmmmhhh...alright...yes, sir...they're right here. Is the plane ready? Send them over, got it...yes, I will do so right away."

She smiled again and pointed down the long hallway. "I'm so sorry I can't guide you. I'm very busy right now. We moved the plane, but it should be easy to find. It's in Terminal A. I'm sure you know where that is, Mr. Adam?"

"Yes, ma'am." Adam beckoned us to follow him, and as we walked away I heard Marla dialing another number. She began speaking in that sharp voice once again. I turned around just to look at her one last time; I liked her; and thought I saw someone duck behind a plant as I turned. I doubted it was anyone of significance, and turned back to follow the others. I had an apology to make.

"Cameron?" I barely noticed Marc's expression as I hurried up to Cameron and tapped him on the shoulder.

"Cameron, I'm really sorry. I know I said you were a traitor, but I realize now it's not true. You've done so much for us...will you forgive me?"

"Yeah. I know how you must have felt...I'd have thought the same thing." I looked into Cameron's bright eyes and smiled.

"Thanks," I whispered. Then I sighed, knowing a quite large burden had just been taken off my shoulders. Unfortunately, Marc had noticed my gaze when I looked up at Cameron, and I don't think he was too happy about it. But there was nothing I could do. If he was jealous, he was jealous. I'd admit it. I really did like Cameron.

The plane was smaller than the other one, but not by too much, and it was older and rusty. I had been wrong - that plane was *NOT* better than the other. No wonder it had been a back-up plan. If only I didn't make things so hard and complicated.

Griffin and Adam made sure us kids stayed out of their way while they checked the plane for damage, and when they gave us the all clear, we stepped into it. We crawled to the back and sat down hastily. Griffin looked extremely excited and jacked up, and we didn't want to get in his way. Especially me. His emotions were so strong that they were flowing like an ocean current at me. They weren't as strong as the last time, but they were different and strong nonetheless.

We buckled and got comfortable, and Adam began switching different dials on and off, on and off. They started the engine, the motor. A loud buzzing filled my ears. In a matter of minutes we were rolling down the runway, gaining speed and going faster and faster. I'd never gone that fast in my life. It was thrilling, and exciting. And then I saw the car, practically flying down the road behind us.

It was so small I could barely make out who was in it. Yet there was only one person it could be...only one car...Ben. He must have known Griffin was going to set off that morning, and after realizing we were gone, not knowing where Griffin might take us, he had decided to wait until morning to come find us at the airport. He was definitely smart. And brave, for trying to drive a car like Andria's. He looked like some drunk, reckless guy driving that fast. But luckily it was only him and no police.

"Go faster! We need to lift off NOW!" Griffin cried, mortified to find that Ben was coming to our rescue. His face distorted in rage, he jammed his finger at a couple of buttons and we rocketed into the sky. I screamed, and clutched for Marc sitting beside me. He wrapped his arms around me tightly.

It all seemed to be worse than skydiving, and there I was probably safer. Yet when we slowed, I realized how wonderful it really was. It gave me a whole new perspective of the sky, of the clouds! How could you live in a place like Pastel or Scharr and never experience those wonders? It really did amaze me.

We lifted higher and higher until my ears began to pop. Cameron handed me a piece of minty gum and I chewed as hard as I could to get the popping to stop. Marc chewed some too, all the while glancing out the window and concentrating.

"Are you ready?" he whispered. Cameron and I nodded, but Marc only raised his eyebrows. "Let me re-phrase that - Creed, are you ready?" Cameron narrowed his eyes and leaned over me.

"What do you think you're doing? I'm going too!"

"NO, YOU'RE NOT!" Marc said this so forcefully that both of us flinched back. "I'm sorry, Cameron, really, but how are you going to get back to your parents? If the King or anyone else in Pastel finds you, you'll never be able to leave again."

Cameron glared at Marc. He gritted his teeth and clenched his fists and glared harder. Then he relaxed. "Fine. I won't go. But I have to do something first."

He leaned over and kissed me. I felt a warmth spread through my body, and then I shivered. Was it possible to be hot and cold at the same time? I looked at him, and he flushed bright red. Marc quivered with anger and rage. He unbuckled me roughly and pushed me as far away from Cameron as I would go. Then he squeezed between us.

"Are you ready?"

"Yes. Bye, Cameron. Thanks so much." I tried to give Cameron the best face I could, an expression showing all of my thanks, gratitude, sadness, and fright for his fate at the same time. Marc held my hand and we dropped down to the floor. If Griffin or Adam saw us, we'd be dead. Worse than that, maybe.

We made our way between two seats and crawled to the door in the side of the plane.

Marc glanced out one of the windows and pointed out a large cloud right below.

I nodded to show I understood, and then everything after that was a blur. It happened so quickly, and now it comes back to me in small clips of memory:

Cameron shouting and stumbling behind us, the pudgy fingers of Fabia grabbing me from behind, Marc yanking open the plane door, Griffin and Adam glancing back at us from their chairs, Griffin's cry of anguish, defeat, and hatred. The emotions of everyone around me clogged my air and almost suffocated me, and I probably would've fainted if it hadn't been for the jump.

For the second time of my life, I was free falling through the sky. Once again with three people, one of them a different person. Fabia had followed us; out of the house, into the car, into the airport, into the plane, and then out the window. And she was clinging to my back as if there were no tomorrow. The extra weight dragged us down.

I thought I could still hear the screams of the people in the plane above us, dive-bombing right past us to try and find us. Griffin's bellowing, Adam's tears for his daughter, and Cameron's cries of fright. But the air soon sucked them up and we were left in utter silence.

Inside of me, somewhere, deep, deep down, I guess I had known all along that Marc really did have a plan. Not an escape plan, no. But a plan to return to our rightful home. Not to the home of Adam, Eloisa, and Fabia, or the home of Andria, Griffin, Cameron, and soon to be Rocco. Not to the home of the wildlife in the Apennines or Alps mountains, but to my home, our home, in Pastel.

"*OOMMMPPPHHH!*" I hit something soft, yet hard and dense at the same time. Fabia began to sob into my arms, and I sat up and patted her gently. Marc sat beside me, gazing around in awe.

That's when I realized we weren't...well, anywhere. We were still in the sky, sitting in the sky as if there were an invisible floor. But when I looked down, it wasn't invisible. The cloud beneath us was as real and life-like as anything I'd ever seen. It was so fluffy, so soft, so warm and cuddly. Still clutching tightly to Fabia, and her to me, I layed down on it and sighed. I pulled off some of it's edges, like cotton candy, and pressed them together flat into a blanket. Then, sliding Fabia off me gently, I wrapped the blanket around her and sang her a soft lullaby.

"Go to sleep...go to sleep...go to sleep sweet Fabia...you'll find comfort...in this sky...with the cloud surrounding you." I sang the song twice, and she sighed in complete fatigue.

Once I was sure she was asleep, I turned to Marc and changed my gentle expression completely.

"*What* were you *thinking*? *That* was your plan? To jump out of the plane and hope that some theory was correct? And hope that...*Oh, maybe we'll live after all!* NO! It doesn't work like that! And if this theory hadn't worked, we'd be responsible for *killing* Fabia!" I gulped some fresh air into my lungs before going on. "I don't fancy becoming a MURDERER!"

Marc laughed. "We're not murderers."

"That's right. We *aren't*. But we *could* have been." Marc only laughed again.

"Whatever. Now how do we steer this thing? We can't live here. We've got to get back up to Pastel."

"*YOU THINK?!*" I shouted so loudly that poor Fabia twitched in her sleep. I felt so bad for her. What had we done?

"Well, if you think my ideas are so bad all of a sudden, let's hear yours about her." Marc jabbed a finger at Fabia, almost blaming me for having her with us. It wasn't my fault she had been smart enough to see where we were going so early in the morning.

"I don't have any ideas other than the fact that she has to stay with us and we can't let her out of our sight."

"YOU THINK?" Marc mimicked. It reminded me so much of what it had been like back when we were little that I laughed, long and hard. I hadn't laughed since who knew when.

Marc smiled, and we looked around again. The sky was crystal blue, and other than the white clouds floating around us, it was the only color we could see. The cloud drifted upwards, and we both sucked in our breath. Maybe we could just float up to Pastel. That would be fun...yet it seemed too easy. Nothing was 'just easy' anymore.

We sat on the cloud enjoying the scenery for a while, and then I got an idea. Maybe we could shape some of the cloud into an oar, like I had done with the blanket. We could even make the cloud into a boat!

I was glad we had remembered our packs. With excited, trembling fingers, I opened Marc's pack and took out the rope he had brought. Finding a paper clip at the very bottom, I attached it to the rope, bent it so that it was long and pointy with a sort of hook on the end, and began to fish for another cloud. I'd throw the rope out into the sky, and if it hooked onto another cloud, I'd rein it in and we'd mold it into a small ball. Once we had five balls, I stopped cloud-fishing and we focused on molding our cloud into a boat. We turned up the edges and patted them into place. It turned out looking like a sort of bathtub instead of a canoe or boat. But that was okay. We had done well.

The oar came next. We molded the small balls into two very flat, fluffy sticks, and then flattened them to look like oars. When we plunged them into the air around the boat, we were able to propel it forward. Since we had no idea where our city was, we assumed it was up. So that was the direction we headed.

At one point, since it was pretty hard to go up using oars, we had to cloud-fish and get Marc another cloud. He had to climb into it himself and push us upwards. It was slow going, but we were actually doing alright. For the very first time in what seemed like years, I wasn't worried. About anything.

♦ ♦ ♦

An Unhappy Ending

Ryn had the illness her mother had gotten before she died. The illness that hadn't gone away. Of course, Queen Celeste had the illness much worse, but Katheryn had it too, and Helen had figured her days were numbered.

"Not necessarily," the doctor said. "Katheryn really only has a mild case of the disease, though it may not seem like it, and once it's come out of hiding it stays with you for life. I doubt it will get any worse than this, yet I'm sure it will drain her energy quite frequently."

"What can we do, doctor?" Helen had tried to keep the tears out of her eyes, but her attempts failed. The doctor looked at her sympathetically.

"I'll give her a prescription and order her a wheelchair. It will make it much easier for her to get around."

"Thank you! But what about...how will she...?"

"But what about being Queen, you ask? I don't know. I suggest filling her in and letting her decide." Helen groaned. "You weren't planning on doing that?" The doctor asked incredulously. Helen looked away guiltily. "You can't keep it from her much longer, sweet." With that, he walked away, leaving Helen standing in the hallway trying to figure out a way to break the bad news to her sister, who was lying in bed in her room.

When Helen walked through the door, Katheryn saw her expression and tried to cheer her up.

"Come on! It's not that bad, is it? I'm getting better, right?"

Helen burst into tears. What was she to do? Katheryn beckoned her over and patted the space beside her in the bed. Helen climbed in and snuggled next to her, somewhat relieved. Katheryn put her arm around her and comforted her, and it worked a little. But every time Helen let her mind wander, she came back to the illness and let another set of tears flow. Every time this happened Katheryn just hugged her tighter. Finally, when Ryn thought she couldn't possibly stand it any longer, she whispered,

"Tell me, Helen." Helen fell silent, and looked up into Katheryn's eyes. She sighed.

"You have *the* illness, Ryn. Mom's disease."

Katheryn was quiet.

"He's sure?"

"Positive. He's ordering you a wheelchair and is getting you a prescription."

"So...I'm not going to...die?"

"Not anytime soon."

"Good." Katheryn propped herself up and stared out into space. "It's genetic, right? I've had it all of my life and it's never shown itself before?"

"Apparently."

The girls were silent once more. Katheryn looked like she was thinking - hard. There must have been several thoughts whirring around her mind, as there were for Helen. But she did not voice them aloud. No, she remained silent, and when she did finally say something, it shocked Helen so completely that she forgot all of those thoughts in her head and almost fainted.

"There's only one thing left to do, Helen," she paused, "We'll make you Queen."

♦ ♦ ♦

Scharr

The city came into sight just as the sky around us was darkening. That was good news, because we wouldn't have had any light at all if we were still floating during the night. It was so strange to see our city again after spending so many months Down Below. I felt like we'd grown, matured, and I was sure the city had, too. It was so unfamiliar that something inside me stirred, and awakened. I didn't want to admit that it may have been fear. At least I wasn't alone; for I could feel Marc's emotions stirring inside of him, too. I didn't want to embarrass him, so I didn't say anything.

We paddled up, up, up until we were level with the very bottom of the city. The gates towered above me, and something looked sinister about them. If it wasn't just the night sky playing tricks on me, then Pastel must have changed very much. I gulped just thinking about it.

"Wake Fabia."

"No, I'd rather wait until we've gone inside," I said quietly, never taking my eyes off of those gates.

"Yes, that might be smarter." Marc didn't take his eyes off the gates, either.

We didn't say another word until the cloud was just beside the entrance. I had just stepped onto the soft cloud ground when Marc pulled my arm. This time, he looked so grim I just had to ask him why he was so scared.

"What's wrong?" I whispered.

"Creed! Look at the gates." Marc was barely speaking. But we had had so much practice mouthing to each other that it was almost as if I could hear his voice. I turned slowly and almost fainted. The gates did not read Pastel, as they were supposed to. Instead, they read:

Scharr

Things had gone wrong before, but nothing as wrong as that. We had read many a passage in Cecily's journal describing Scharr, and even though it was her home, she hated it at the same time. She said it was a prison - a place of misery and punishment and horror. From what we had gathered about Cecily, she was a bit dramatic, but no one could be *that* dramatic. Yes, we were beginning to believe Scharr was an evil place. Imagine that. Of all places.

"Let's leave." I tried to get back into the boat, but Marc stopped me. "What's your problem?" I asked, annoyed. "Do you want to leave or do you, for some crazy reason, want to stay here?"

Marc looked at as if to say: Get a clue, Creed.

"Hello? Cecily lives here. Cecily! The one who was swapped; kidnapped; at birth? Remember?"

My guilty conscience understood what Marc was saying, but my heart and soul didn't want to believe him. So I asked anyway, "What about her?"

I winced when he yelled at me, perhaps too loudly.

"We should *rescue* her, what else?" I reddened, and turned around so Marc wouldn't see. I had such a dark heart. How could I have wanted to leave so soon? We had a mission to accomplish.

We woke up Fabia, and Marc broke off some of his rope and tethered our make-shift boat to one of the bars of Scharr's gate.

Fabia shivered with fright when I told her what she had to do. I hated doing it to her, but if we were going to rescue Cecily, someone had to do it. And Marc and I were too big. I took her by the shoulders and looked into her wide, innocent eyes.

"Please?" I asked.

She ducked her head and hid her face in a curtain of straight brown hair. I lifted her chin and hugged her close. "Please?" I whispered into her hair. She nodded, her cheeks tear stained, and bravely stepped between two of the gate's bars. She was so tiny that she fit perfectly. She barely even had to squeeze.

Once on the other side, she glanced behind her apprehensively and looked at us. She asked something in Italian, and Marc answered.

"What did she say?" I asked.

"She wanted to know what to do next. I told her to find a switch or something to open the gate."

"I wonder if there are any guards? It seems unlikely that there wouldn't be."

"I know." Marc gazed around inquiringly. Then he gulped. I hated when he did that. Couldn't he just tell me what was wrong instead of staring straight ahead as if he'd seen a ghost? "I bet there are security cameras! Darn it, I wish Cameron would've let us take Cecily's journal! If only we could have read up on her security system! There was an entire passage on it, you know."

I gulped, too. We were definitely in a tight spot. I peeked through the bars and tried to spot little Fabia. I hoped no

one had seen her. Just then, there was a loud *creek*. I stepped
back just in time before the gates opened out. Cautiously, we
walked inside. There was Fabia. She was smiling
triumphantly, and standing next to a small box in the stone
wall. It was open to reveal a series of complex buttons and
knobs. One was marked 'gate'. Fabia must have been so
proud of herself for reading English!

I ran over to her and swooped her up in a big hug. She
weighed no more than a light feather. Marc walked over and
smiled at her, too. Then he began talking in rapid Italian.

"Si!" was Fabia's exuberant reply. With a grunt, Marc
lifted her onto his back and we began our walk into the city.
The gates closed silently behind us.

We trudged onwards, though we were tired as could be.
The buildings were so desolate, so lonely and tall and
sinister. The name fit the city well. It was as if it had been a
beautiful city at one point - and then something tragic
happened and all was left of the city and the sadness was a
scar - a scab, a cut, one healing painfully over time.

I hated the fact that it was night, but I guessed it was for
the best. We wouldn't have wanted anyone to see us
sneaking in. Nevertheless, they probably would; if there
were security cameras. We'd have to rescue Cecily and make
a quick getaway if we were to stay alive for much longer. Or
worse - we would all be locked up. But before I thought of
even graver possibilities, I reminded myself that we were
there to set something straight - we were here for the good
of Cecily and any others harmed by "O Evil One."

"I think we need to rest," Marc whispered. I nodded
wearily and we ducked into a narrow alleyway behind a
couple of shops. We made a wall of garbage cans, and then
took out the delicate pieces of cloud we had packed. We

molded them into pillows and a big blanket, and quietly lay down to rest.

In the morning, I awoke to a ray of light shining in my eyes and several faces looking down at me.

"Mornin', sunshine! I thought you'd *never* wake up." A plump woman was bending down so far over me that I could feel her breath on my face. When I rolled over, only Fabia was still beside me. The cloud we had been using for pillows and a blanket were gone...as was Marc. I sat up abruptly and bunked heads with the woman. She yelped in pain.

"Gosh, Anita, that ought to teach you not to get so close to people in the future!" I turned and saw yet another face. Another woman was bending over me, but she wasn't as close as Anita had been. Anita rubbed her head and stuck her face into the other woman's.

"I can do whatever I like, Miss Priss!" Apparently she could, for she was, once again, as close to the woman as she had been to me. I felt bad for the other woman.

"Get out of my face, Anita! Goodness, sometimes I feel like punching that close nose of yours!"

Anita stumbled backwards and lost her footing, and she tumbled to the ground. Miss Priss paid no attention to her, and with her nose in the air, she stomped through the back door of a shop.

"Don't listen to Emmeline. She's far too strict." Anita pulled herself up and offered me a hand. I took it, and then woke Fabia. She glanced around, wild eyed, and I picked her up into my arms.

"Excuse me? Have you seen my friend?" I asked. My voice wasn't as brave as I had intended it to be.

"You bet. Tough kid. He's inside trying to bargain with my husband." Anita rolled her eyes and lumbered through the same door Emmeline had just disappeared into. I followed closely. I wanted to ask what Marc was bargaining over, but I didn't dare once I saw the scene in front of me.

Marc and some old man were seated at a creaky old table in the center of the room. They were face to face, having a very heated discussion. Our presence didn't seem to matter to them. They barely even noticed.

"Sir! I'm sorry, but I don't have anything to offer you. However, we really need a place to stay, and your wife here says it's a bad idea to be sleeping outside in these parts."

The old guy grunted and ran his fingers through his graying hair. He laughed, and glanced up at Anita. Marc was going through our packs, I assumed to try and find something worth trading.

"Son...Marc, did you say?...I know you need a place to stay, but we do, too, and if we don't make an income while letting beggars like yourself sleep here for free...we'll go broke! I simply can't do it." He got up from the table, a sure sign that the conversation was over. But Marc cleared his throat and the man turned. He looked genuinely annoyed; I was sure no other kid had ever challenged him like Marc was; but he sat down again anyway. "What do you want? One last chance."

"Alright. How about this? We don't want to stay for long. If we're good, and we help cook or clean or something, we stay."

There was silence around the table. Marc raised his eyebrows and leaned back, trying to look content. But the anxiousness in his eyes was so clear to me that I was practically positive the old man could see it, too.

"You have a deal. By the way, call me Cole." He smiled, and shook hands with Marc. Anita looked down at me and grinned.

"Come on, kids. We'll find you a room." By then I had realized we weren't in a shop. Luck had led us to an inn, one of the best cheap inns you could find in the whole city, Cole claimed.

We were led to a tiny room with two cots. I figured I'd have to share with Fabia. It was okay; she was so tiny anyway. The cots were tiny, too, with ragged sheets and dirty covers. The pillows had been fluffed, but were stained and kind of smelly. There was barely any furniture, but it was free, and it would have to do.

Besides, I didn't think Marc wanted to stay there during the day anyway. All we'd need it for would be to sleep, and that was only at night. I sighed, and after plopping my pack on the bed, decided against it and picked it up again. Who knew what kind of people stayed there?

Surprisingly, it was a little chilly outside, so I pulled my sweater out of my pack and gave it to Fabia, who'd been shivering ever since we got there. I never let go of her hand, and pulled her along beside me.

"Where should we go first?" I asked Marc as we tiptoed down the stairs. Some of the tenants might still be sleeping.

"I think we should ask Cole and Anita about Cecily first."

I nodded and we approached them as soon as we reached the first floor. They were setting the table and cooking for breakfast. We each got a plate of eggs and sat down at the long dining table.

"Thank you very much, Cole, Anita. Just let us know when you'd like us to begin work. We have some errands to run today, but we'll return at any time you may need us."

"Good. We'll need you today at lunch and dinner. You can help set the table, cook, clean, and wash the dishes. It won't be any extra trouble coming back, for you have to eat anyway. Does that sound fair to you?" Anita wiped her large, plump hands on her apron and smiled.

Marc and I looked at each other, then shook our heads yes. We didn't want to make a fuss.

Nonchalantly, after chewing a bite of eggs, Marc looked up from his plate and asked,

"Do you guys have any idea where a certain Cecily lives? Her father is Elias...?"

Anita froze and dropped the plate she had been wiping. It clattered to the floor and broke into tiny pieces. She stared down at them and hesitated before she went to get a broom.

Once she was done cleaning, she gazed at Marc and said,

"Young man. You don't know where Cecily LaFlore lives? Her father is probably the richest man in the entire city! Besides the King, of course."

"Ummmm...no, we knew she was rich...we just...need to find out where she lives."

"Right. Let me find the address for you. It's a very large house, a mansion, really. Elias is a doctor. He's studying to be a lawyer, too, and right now he's the best doctor in the city. His daughter is quite snippy, but sweet, too, and by gosh she's smart. Elias jokes that she actually tries to run away. It seems funny - what would a girl like her want to run away for? She should be grateful that she lives that lifestyle!"

We laughed and murmured our agreement, while we were really trying to communicate without speaking.

"You know, it's funny! You look just like her! What did you say your name was again?" Anita turned to look at me. I giggled nervously.

"Oh. Ummmm...My name is Creed. We're here to..."

"...Tour this part of the city. We've heard many things about Cecily LaFlore." Marc finished for me. I sighed. That was a close one. I mean, I was positive I would've come up with something, but how long would that have taken? I wasn't necessarily one to think on my feet. Anita nodded and looked away thoughtfully. I hoped she wasn't too suspicious of us. It would probably do us some good to get away from the inn before she questioned me more.

We left a couple of minutes later, down the streets of Scharr and trying to find the right roads. Scharr sure was different than Pastel. It was so eerie, so dark and mysterious. The towers loomed up overhead, slick and with no texture. The only colors Scharr seemed to use in construction were gray, black, and white.

The people were the same: Gray, black, and white. There was no originality, no creativity or excitement. The people lived dull, routine lives. The prison was scary. Our prison was just a small building on the outskirts of the city, surrounded by the King's guards.

This prison was the tallest tower in Scharr. It rose high above the others, sleek and slender. It was so high I could barely even count the floors, but I did reach 36. There were no windows, and I wondered how they could get air in such a safe place like that. The double doors were guarded by four guards, and they were heavily padlocked with locks the size of baseballs. Thick, steel bars covered the door.

The guards had grim expressions, and even from where we stood I could feel their sickly emotions. They wore red-hot tunics and pants black as night. A small fire was sewn onto the tunic's front, and a lightening bolt danced in it's flames. The bolt reminded me of the city's name: Scharr.

We passed many more grim guards, and each time they squinted at us as if they could see right through to the truth. Marc had just guided us into a dim alleyway, trying to follow Anita's tiny handwriting, when he slammed us against the wall of a building. He put a finger to his lips and turned around slowly. Standing in the entrance to the alleyway were four boys, taller and much stronger than Marc.

"Who are you?" one asked darkly.

"Well...ummm...we're....ummm...just looking for someone."

"Oh really? And where are you from?" another asked sarcastically. He smiled, and the four stepped closer. I looked into their four faces and concentrated. They knew something we didn't. Had they seen us enter Scharr? I had a feeling I already knew the answer.

Marc gulped, and I could practically hear his heart beating loudly inside his chest. He was trying his best to be brave.

"We're orphans," he said loudly, and pressed harder against me. I held Fabia to my chest. She was soaking my shirt with her tears, but luckily she was smart enough to know not to make a sound.

The four guys moved closer. I could see almost every line in their faces, every hair on their heads...I could smell their putrid breath.

Nobody moved for at least one full second. Then Marc stood up and punched the closest kid...hard. He wore an expression new to me. One I'd never seen before. He pushed his hair back and grimaced at the kid. The guy staggered back, holding his nose. When he took his hand away, it was covered in blood. I squeezed my eyes shut and tried not to watch the ugly fight unfolding before me. The other three boys were mad. It was obviously because they'd just been hit by some younger kid. Marc punched at one of the others, and missed. The one with the bloody nose growled and delivered a shockingly hard punch to Marc's eye. I couldn't keep my eyes closed much longer. I watched as Marc's eye began to turn purple. Fabia was sobbing loudly now, not still and silent like before. I felt bad for her. It was partly my fault she was there. Slowly and quietly, I pushed her away from me and let her fall to the floor. While Marc kept the guys occupied, I snuck up from behind and delivered my own punch. It came in contact with the closest kid, one of the biggest, and he turned to look at me. I punched him in the stomach. For some strange reason, it felt good.

"Quit it you little TWIRP!" The eldest boy, most likely the worst, reached out to grab me. He was able to trip me once, and was leaning down to do some damage, but was stopped abruptly when Marc gave him a kick between the legs. He yowled and hopped backwards against the opposite wall. The other boys glared at Marc and cautiously went over to their leader to see if he was okay.

The boys turned around. Advancing, they asked,

"Who do you need to see? You'd better get your business done quickly, because we're taking you to jail. We don't like trespassers."

They snorted and high-fived each other.

"Come on. Let's go," Marc said. The guys barely had time to take another step towards us before we heard a voice.

"I'm assuming they're here to see me?"

All seven of us whipped around. Including Fabia, who had recovered herself and was leaning against the wall. You had to admit, she was a pretty brave child. Not to mention curious.

Leaning against the wall of the alley was a girl about my age. She looked a lot like me. She had wavy blond hair that fell just an inch below her shoulders, and eyes that sparkled. Her mouth was twisted into a sly smile, and her clothes identified her as an obvious tomboy. I knew her immediately. The girl was Cecily LaFlore.

"Are...are you?" the boys stuttered, amazed. They glanced back and forth between us; Cecily, us, Cecily, us.

"Duh," I answered. Then I held my head up high and pulled Fabia along with me. We walked right past the four boys to go stand by Cecily. She smiled at me and gave me a high five behind her back. Marc followed us a second later, after rubbing a hand over his swelling eye.

"Leave them alone from now on, Anik. You and your little friends." Cecily waved a hand and after glancing back at us one last time, they left. Gone.

"How did you know we wanted to see you?" I asked quietly.

"I didn't. Anik likes to have 'fun' with everyone. They really only listen to me, and if I don't want half-dead people walking around my neighborhood, I stop them."

"Oh," I said. Cecily was just like I had imagined her. Short and to the point. Sarcastic. Funny. Brave.

"So, who are you? I've never seen you around before. I'm Cecilia LaFlore. Call me..."

"Cecily?" I asked before she could finish. She looked at me strangely.

"Yeah. How did you know? Most think I'd like to be called Cilia."

"Well..." I looked at Marc. He rubbed his eye. Then he nodded. "Well, we know all about you. Sort of. Even though we don't live here or anything." I was trying to phrase my words in the right way without giving anything away too quickly. But I should have known. That was the way Cecily liked things.

"You don't live here?" she asked quietly.

"No." I looked at my shoes and stroked Fabia's hair before going on. "We...it's a long story, but...we know the person who found your journal, and we...well, we read some of it."

"Do you believe it?" Cecily was practically hopping up and down in excitement.

"Yes." I nodded, and she gripped me in a tight bear hug.

"I don't need explanations. Let's get out of here. I'm going to go get some things, and I'll meet you at the inn down the street." We knew where that was. We hurried down the alleyway towards it, glancing about the whole way to be sure Anik didn't want any more "fun."

While we waited, we helped Anita and Cole get ready for lunch. We didn't have to wait long. Cecily arrived about five minutes later, a sack slung over her back. She smiled and waved to Anita and Cole, and set a $50.00 bill on the table in front of them.

"For their room," she explained. Then we hurried outside and ran through the city to the gates. As we ran, I saw something flash golden in the light on Cecily's wrist. We didn't have time for me to see what it was. We had to get out of Scharr as fast as we could.

When we reached the gate, four guards and Anik and his friends were already there, sick grins spread across their faces.

"We put two and two together, Cecily," Anik laughed. "Your story and theirs." He looked at us for a split second before falling back with the four other guards. "There is no way we're letting you out of this city."

I groaned. Marc groaned. We'd had enough of everything. We weren't even nervous or scared anymore...it was almost as if we had been expecting it. Cecily just glared. She had a wonderful death stare.

"Anik, I was kidnapped at birth. I've been stuck in this rat's nest for the last 13 years of my life. I'm not about to make it 14. I am leaving this wretched city - right here, right now."

The guards stiffened.

"Move, Anik. Step away from the gate."

"Nice try. Not this time, sport. I realized I shouldn't let a little 13 year old boss me around. I did in the past because I was afraid of your father. He could rearrange my face so that no doctor could fix it."

I couldn't believe it. But hadn't it seemed too easy anyway? Cecily didn't seem to think so. She took a bold step forward and tried to kick the head guard. He caught her leg as if that kind of thing happened every day. He didn't let go and leaned into Cecily's face. His breath reached her nostrils and she gagged.

"How did you think you were going to get away anyway?" He smiled. She looked down at her shoes; the guard had just released her leg.

"I...I'm not sure." She gulped and looked bravely into his face. "Punishment?" She asked.

"Your regular. The ultimate." Cecily groaned.

"I don't want to clean!" She tried to yank herself away, and in the split second that she was turned to us, she winked and let a quick smile escape. Obviously she could think quickly on her feet like Marc.

The other guards, on a signal from the head man, marched over to us and grabbed us by the arms. Their tunics were so bright they burned my eyes. My guard was the largest. He squeezed my arm so hard I was sure he had cut off all blood flow. I remembered how that had happened at the airport and realized I probably should work on my strength.

The guards *actually* opened the gate and led us outside. I hadn't seen the platform the night before, but I did then. There was a ledge surrounding the entire city, and you could crouch there against the wall. They shoved us onto the ledge and handed us toothbrushes.

"Get cleaning!" they barked. "We're not going to be here in person, but boy, you can bet your bottom dollar we're watching! There are security cameras all over the place!" They separated us until we were spread out on the ledge. I crouched down and dipped the toothbrush into the bucket of soap they had given me. Then I scrubbed. The stones were so large that it would take me at least half an hour to clean one of them! No wonder they called it the ultimate punishment.

I had been scrubbing for 10 minutes before Cecily was able to make her way over to me. Still scrubbing hard, she whispered,

"What's the plan? You guys wouldn't have suggested leaving if you didn't have a way to leave. Besides, how did you get here if you don't live here?"

I bit my lip and held up my finger. Then I looked down the row at Marc. He was already looking at me. 'Ready?' I mouthed. He nodded. I gestured for him to hurry up, and he grabbed Fabia and whispered something in her ear. Then they began crawling down the ledge towards us.

I looked around for our cloud. Luckily, the guards hadn't seen it because it had floated under the city floor. They had failed to notice the rope, too, which was still tethered to one of the gate bars. Slowly, still scrubbing like Cecily had done, I inched my way over to the bars of the city gate. Our plan would only work if no one saw me. Gently, I pulled the rope and out came the cloud. Then I untied it from the gate and guided it towards Marc. He caught it and pushed Fabia in first. He followed, picked up the oar, and rowed over to us. Cecily's eyes nearly popped out of her head.

"This is amazing!" As she climbed in next to Fabia, I saw the same golden thing glint on her wrist. I looked closer. A golden bracelet. Golden like the sun, shining on her wrist.

"Can I see that?" I asked quietly.

"Sure." Cecily slipped the bracelet off her wrist and handed it to me. I turned it over. Engraved on the back was the name *Cecily*. I gulped. Then I looked up at Cecily, who was staring at me curiously.

"Who are you?" I asked.

"I don't know," she whispered.

But it all made too much sense. She looked nothing like Elias. And every bit like me. The wavy blond hair...the green eyes...gold bracelet. She was abducted at birth, and not from Scharr. If Elias had never been down Below, then the only place he could've kidnapped her from would have been Pastel.

A smile spread over our faces as we stared into each other's eyes. Our sister's eyes.

Lock and Key

Helen stared out over the Wall from her balcony. Creed had to come back sometime; the necklace assured that. Supposing she hadn't lost it.

NO. That thought was not allowed. Helen forced herself to stay positive...although it seemed like nothing could go right these days. First, Creed's escape, second, her father's death, third, Katheryn's illness, and fourth, the fact that there was going to have to be another coronation. Helen loved coronations. She thought they were beautiful and wonderful in every way. But it was another matter when the coronation was for *you* and *you* shouldn't be the one ruling in the first place.

She leaned onto the balcony banister and closed her eyes. When she opened them again, she couldn't believe what she was seeing. She thought her eyes were deceiving her. But after rubbing them again and again, she was forced to believe the sight.

Her heart gave a leap and she hugged herself. She jumped up and down and threw her arms out wide, taking in the sweet smell of the air around her. She was going to be alright. Everything was going to work out after all. Creed, although she barely knew her, would help her rule. Her parents lived at the castle, so she would live there, too, and she would have to help Helen rule. She'd know what to do.

As the Keeper, with the necklace, she would help keep the city safe.

Helen breathed a sigh of relief and felt tears in her eyes. Tears of joy. She felt so good, so free, so wonderful. Maybe she would make a good ruler. Maybe she'd rise to the occasion. If she didn't die or fall ill first.

But she made a pact to herself then and there - she would win the respect of her subjects. They were terrified right now with the news of Katheryn's illness, but she would lift their spirits. She would command their trust and do everything in her power to keep them safe, to keep them happy and without worry. At the moment, she thought she could fly. But then she looked down again.

There was Creed, and her friend Marc. But there were two others. A third was alright; Helen had known Creed and Marc were going with Ben, an older man. But Ben was not sitting with them. There were two other girls. A younger one, clinging to Creed in fright, and another who looked about the same age as Creed, and just like her, too. And what were they riding on? Marc was pulling it through the sky with a white oar, and they were approaching quickly. Helen didn't want anyone to know of their return yet...so she decided not to tell anyone but Creed's parents. She would go tell them immediately...after she watched what the four did.

She ran to the other side of the balcony to keep them in sight. There they rowed; closer and closer until they reached the gate. They stepped out onto the ledge and Marc tied the boat-like-thing to a bar of the gate. Helen held her breath.

Creed shook the bars of the gate and held them. Helen was too far away to see her facial expression. She could only guess at how annoyed she must look. But there...slowly,

Creed reached up and felt her neck. She pulled the necklace out from her shirt and stared at it. She let go of the gate and looked at the tiny, almost invisible, lock on the middle bar. Then she guided the tiny key on her necklace to the lock of Pastel's gates. It was a perfect fit.

About The Author

Brooke has dreamed of publishing a book since she established her love of writing at a very early age. She has written numerous short stories, mysteries, and poems. Brooke has also entered many writing contests, hoping for success. De Couleur Pale (Pastel) is a dream come true for her, and she is already working avidly on the sequel.

Made in the USA
Charleston, SC
19 October 2012